THE ORDEAL

VASILY BYKOV

The Ordeal

Translated from the Russian by
GORDON CLOUGH

NEW YORK
E. P. DUTTON & CO., INC.
1972

First published in the U.S.A. 1972 by E. P. Dutton & Co., Inc.
English translation Copyright © 1972 by Gordon Clough
All rights reserved. Printed in the U.S.A.

FIRST EDITION

First published in Russia as *Sotnikov,* 1970

Library of Congress Catalog Card Number: 77-179837
SBN: 0-525-17195-9

THE ORDEAL

I

The path through the wood was shrouded in a smooth, deadening sheet of snow, and as they walked they could see no trace of hoofmarks, sleigh tracks, or human footprints. Probably, few people passed this way even in the summer, and now, after the heavy February falls, everything was so sheeted in snow that had it not been for the ragged corridor which the firs and alders outlined pale against the night sky, it would have been next to impossible to tell that there was a path here at all. But they were on the right road. As Rybak peered ahead through the leafless underbrush, which the onset of dusk made seem even denser, he recognised more and more of the landmarks he recalled from the previous autumn when he and four others of Smolyakov's group had pushed along this path to the farm for the same reason as now—to get hold of some kind of provisions. Over there he could make out the familiar outline of the small hollow where three of them had sat and smoked waiting for a signal to follow from the two who had gone on ahead. But today there would have been no chance of going down into the hollow; an arching snow-cornice sprang from the rim, and the leafless trees clinging to the valley sides were up to their tops in snow.

The thin sliver of moon which drifted along with them, level, it seemed, with the tops of the fir trees, was a mere flicker of pale light among the cold gleam of the stars. But even so it made the night seem less lonely, as if something alive and unobtrusive was gently keeping them company. Deeper into the forest, the closely clustering firs, the undergrowth, and the ragged shadows cast by the intertwined dead brush made it very dark, but out on the track the pure whiteness of the snow showed up the path with no difficulty at all. It led across virgin land, which made the going harder, but was an insurance against surprise attack; no one could mount an ambush from the thickets. Yet, Ryback was on his guard, especially since they had come through Glinyany, where a couple of hours ago they had all but stumbled on a German patrol. Fortunately, just outside the village, they had come across an old man out gathering firewood. He had warned them of the danger, and they had plunged back into the forest, where they had spent a long time fighting their way through the undergrowth before finally coming back on to the track.

All the same, Rybak was armed, and not greatly disturbed by the prospect of a clash in the forest or out in the open. It was true that he was low on ammunition, but there was nothing to be done about that. The men who had stayed behind in the swamp at Gorely had given him all they could spare from their meagre supply. Apart from the five rounds in his rifle, Rybak had three more magazines clinking together in the pocket of his sheepskin, and Sotnikov had the same. It was a pity they had no grenades—but not to worry, they'd be back in camp by the morning. Or at least they should be. True enough, Rybak felt that the Glinyany incident had held them up and that they should keep pressing on. In the forest itself the snow wasn't deep, and on the path the force of the storm had swept the way clear. But they were being held up by Sotnikov.

All the way through the forest Rybak had heard behind him Sotnikov's muffled cough, sometimes nearer, sometimes further away. Now it had ceased completely, and Rybak broke step and looked behind him. Sotnikov had fallen right back, and Rybak could barely make him out stumbling along in the twilight. Rybak suppressed his impatience and watched for a moment as Sotnikov wearily heaved himself through the snow in his clumsy, worn-out boots, with his head, in a Red Army forage cap pulled right over his ears, untypically downcast. Even at this distance, Rybak could hear his rapid, panting breath, which he couldn't control even when he was standing still.

'How's it going? OK?'

'OK!' Sotnikov waved a weary hand, and settled his rifle more comfortably on his shoulder. 'Far to go yet?'

Before answering, Rybak slowed his pace and looked dubiously at the thickset figure of his companion in his tightly belted, short greatcoat. He already knew that Sotnikov would never admit to exhaustion, that he'd urge himself on—oh, we'll get by somehow—so as to make sure that no one else got his job. What other reason could there be? Sotnikov was proud and stubborn enough for three.

6

He's landed this job partly through pride—by an obstinate refusal to admit that he was sick when the commander was selecting a companion for Rybak. He'd called out two others first—Vdovets and Glushchenko—but Vdovets had just stripped his machine-gun and was in the middle of cleaning it, and Glushchenko pleaded wet feet: he'd been to get water and had gone up to his knees in a bog. Then the commander called Sotnikov out, and he'd got up without a word. Once they were well on their way and Sotnikov was seized by a coughing fit, Rybak asked him why he had kept his mouth shut instead of refusing like the other two. Sotnikov had replied, 'I didn't refuse, simply because they did.' Rybak didn't quite understand that reasoning, but all the same he reckoned that there was nothing serious to worry about. After all, the man was on his feet, and there was no point in worrying about a mere cough—you don't die of colds in wartime. Once they got to the house and had a bit of warmth and a plate of hot potatoes, the illness would cure itself.

'No, not far now,' Rybak said encouragingly, and turned to set off again. But before he could take a step Sotnikov launched into a long burst of deep-seated coughing. In an attempt to control it, he bent double and clapped his hand to his mouth, but the coughing only seemed to intensify.

'Snow! Eat some snow, that'll fix it!' Rybak advised.

Sotnikov struggled with a further access of the tearing cough, scooped up a handful of snow and thrust it into his mouth. The cough did indeed die down a little.

'Hell! I'll have to get rid of this, or I'll burst!'

Rybak scowled with concern, but said nothing, and they moved off.

An evenly spaced line of tracks led off from the hollow towards the track, and Rybak realised that a wolf had gone this way recently. Probably, he, too, was heading for human habitation—no fun in the forest in a frost like this. They changed direction slightly to follow the wolf's trail, which in the grey mist of the night showed up the track clearly, and also indicated where the snow lay thinnest—the wolf knew that infallibly. They were getting near the end of their road now, the farm should soon show up, and the thought of that put Rybak into a new and more cheerful mood.

'That Lyubka's a terrific girl!' he said quietly, without turning round. Sotnikov raised his head.

7

'What?'

'I said there's a girl at the farm. Once you see her, that'll cure your cough.'

'Can't you get your mind off girls?'

Sotnikov was having to make great efforts to keep up. He lowered his head, and bent himself even closer to the ground. It looked as if he was concentrating merely on not missing a step and keeping up the tempo he had forced himself into.

'Well, why not? It'd be good to have something to eat, too!'

But even this reference to food had no effect on Sotnikov, who was falling behind again. Rybak slowed down and looked over his shoulder.

'When I was asleep yesterday, back in the swamp, I had a dream about bread. I dreamt I had a hot loaf stuffed down my shirt. When I woke up, it was just the fire warming me. It made me damned mad!'

'No wonder we dream,' Sotnikov agreed thickly. 'What with living this last week on steamed rye.'

'Even that's run out now. Yesterday Gronsky handed out the last of it.' Rybak fell silent.

Although he was now getting genuinely concerned about Sotnikov, Rybak kept his thoughts to himself. And anyway, now wasn't the time for chatter. They were coming close to the end of the forest, and the track was coming out into the open. Ahead the track had a low line of brushwood on one side, with willow bushes growing in the marsh. Then it turned sharply up a small hill, from where, beyond the alders, they should be able to see the shattered roof of the outhouse. And there, beyond the fence, would be the house and the stables, and the winch over the well. If the winch handle is pointing upwards, then everything's OK, but if the hook is hanging on the framework, that means, get out, strangers in the house. True enough, it was a while back as they hadn't been here since the autumn. They'd been operating in different localities on the far side of the main highway, until hunger and the German patrols had driven them back to the places they'd been chased out of a month earlier.

Now they were nearing the turn in the track. Rybak peered over the brushwood more and more impatiently, but the grey twilight was just as impenetrable as before. Then, for a moment, they walked upwards at the side of the road, following the wolf-tracks. It looked as if the wolf, sensing the nearness of human habitation, had gone slowly and cautiously, moving closer to the bushes. The men climbed the snow slope with just as much caution and lack of haste.

Finally, Rybak reached the top of the hill and immediately thought that he must have been mistaken and that the farm was further on. It quite often happens that some stretches of a road you don't know well slip your memory, and you think of the journey as being shorter than it in fact is. Rybak became even more impatient and quickened his pace, and again Sotnikov began to lag behind. Indeed, Rybak had stopped paying any attention to him. Suddenly, and apparently without cause, he was very alarmed.

There was still no sign of the outhouse in the grey night, nor of any of the other buildings, and the gusting wind carried with it the bitter-sweet stench of burning. At first, Rybak thought he was imagining it, or that it was coming from over towards the forest. He carried on a further hundred paces, trying to make out the snow-covered roofs of the farm buildings through the trees. But there was no sign of the farm. And then there was the smell of burning again—not a fresh smell of fire or smoke, but the foul stench of chilled cinders and ashes. Realising that he had made no mistake, Rybak cursed under his breath and, almost at a trot, hurried down the track until he nearly stumbled against the fence.

The fence was still standing, although it had been broken, its two upper rails smashed. Some of the interwoven strands of creeper which had held it together were twisted in the snow. It was here, by the potato clamp, that the outhouse used to stand. Now there was nothing but a snow-covered mound, with here and there what could have been half-burnt-out timbers showing dark against the white. Further away, near the young apple trees, where the farm buildings used to be, there were some more snow-covered hummocks, with the stove, half destroyed but still standing, looking ridiculously naked in their midst. Where the stables had been there was nothing—not even ashes and cinders remained.

For a moment Rybak stood by the fence, a stream of curses churning in his mind. He couldn't think what to do next. The picture he had had before him all the way through the forest came unbidden to his eyes—the house with its simple peasant warmth and comfort, old Malania fussing round the stove in the cottage, baking cakes, and he and Sotnikov, boots off, stretching their feet to the warmth and flirting with that chatterbox Lyubka, while she fed them titbits of dried mushrooms from the forest.

9

Sotnikov came up and stood beside Rybak. He took in what had happened at his first glance, and stood silently looking at what had been the farm buried under the snow. He had another short coughing fit. Rybak finally pulled himself together, stepped over the fence and crossed the yard to the stove, which was topped with a fresh cap of snow. It looked ridiculous standing there, covered in snow, which lay in an unbroken sheet on the top and even blocked the fireplace. The stove-pipe had disappeared, probably fallen off during the fire and lying now under the snow with the rest of the charred remains of the house.

'The swine!' Rybak cursed again.

Sotnikov followed him across the unmarked snow of the yard. He shoved an empty wooden pail aside with the toe of his boot and walked past the wheelless hulk of a half-buried cart. There was nothing else to relieve the eye. Everything the fire had left undevoured must have been looted. The farm had gone, and there was no one left. There wasn't even the trace of a human footprint—the only sign of life was the chain of wolf-tracks outside the fence; even the wolves had a low opinion of this farmstead.

'The bastards, the bastards!' Rybak spat out.

'Someone must have informed on them,' Sotnikov muttered huskily from the well. He had propped himself up against the framework of the winch. He seemed to have shrunk from the cold, and in the intervals of his coughing a quiet, creaky wheeze came from his chest, sounding something like an out-of-tune accordion. Rybak was silent for a while, then thrust his hand into his pocket and, from among the cartridges, fished out a handful of steamed rye, the remains of today's ration.

'D'you want some?'

His companion stretched out his hand a little unwillingly, and Rybak poured some of his rye into it. They silently swallowed the soft cold grains.

'They've destroyed everything!'

Rybak realised that they were now running severely out of luck, and began to suspect that their misfortune was something more than mere chance. It didn't matter all that much that they themselves were hungry—he was far more disturbed by the thought of the men who were freezing out there in the swamp. They were exhausted after a week of fighting and dodging the enemy, they had grown thin on a diet of one potato a day and no bread, and four were wounded, two of them stretcher cases. And now the *politsai*—the renegade Russian militia—and the German police had sealed off the area so effectively that no escape routes remained. Only the swamp region was still open, but there was nowhere to go from there—three kilometres further on there was a village with a garrison, police and road patrols, and it was in wide open country with no forest shelter—no welcome there for a band of partisans.

When he had finished his rye, Rybak looked appraisingly at Sotnikov.

'Well, how d'you feel? If you're bad, you'd better set off back. And I'll slip into the village.'

'On your own?'

'So what? We can't go back empty-handed.'

Sotnikov said nothing, just shivered slightly from the cold; a fierce frost was coming in on the wind. So as to preserve what dregs of warmth he had, he thrust his hands even deeper into the wide sleeves of his greatcoat.

'You won't get warm that way,' Rybak reproached him. 'Why haven't you got hold of a fur hat?'

'Fur hats don't grow on trees.'

'Still, every man in the village has got one.'

Sotnikov paused, then said, 'So you suggest I just steal one from a peasant?'

'No need to steal. There are other ways.'

'All right, let's go.' Sotnikov broke off the conversation.

They climbed back over the fence into the open field. Sotnikov immediately hunched himself up, plunged his head, looking small in its forage cap, deeper into his collar, and tried to turn away from the wind as he walked. Out of the front of his sheepskin Rybak dragged a stained, creased towel, shook it out and turned to Sotnikov.

'Here, wrap this round your neck,' he said. 'You'll feel warmer.'

'Oh, I'm all right.'

'Come on. It'll make a hell of a difference.'

Sotnikov unwillingly stopped, gripped his rifle between his knees, and with stiff, frozen fingers wound the towel round his neck.

'Fine!' said Rybak approvingly. 'Now let's get moving to Guzaki. It's only a couple of kilometres. We'll try to get hold of something, somehow or other.'

2

It was much colder out in the open than it had been in the shelter of the trees. Although the frost-laden wind was not strong, it nagged at them, and no matter how Sotnikov thrust his ungloved hands deep into his pockets, his sleeves or the breast of his greatcoat, they grew stiffer and more painful. In conditions like this, it wouldn't take long for a face—especially ears—to get frostbitten, and he had to keep the circulation going by rubbing his ears with the coarse cloth of his sleeve. He wasn't concerned about his feet—walking kept them warm enough. It was true that he had lost feeling in two toes of his right foot, but that always happened when it froze—they would start to hurt when the thaw set in. But his whole body throbbed painfully from his cold, and today, on top of that, he was beginning to get feverish.

Fortunately out in the open the snow was firm enough and not too deep, so that they were able to keep on the surface almost all the time and their feet broke through the frozen crust only occasionally. They kept close to the field edge which was marked by a fringe of weeds sticking through the snow, and two sets of uneven tracks trailed behind them back into the darkness. It was lighter out here than in the forest, the area of grey shadowy twilight stretched further, and here and there they could see frozen, dried-up blades of sparse grass trembling in the wind. From time to time they came across a sapling standing alone, and after they had been going for a quarter of an hour they spotted a copse of willow or alder in the hollow by the river.

Sotnikov was beginning to feel dreadful. His head was spinning, and sometimes it felt as if something had given way, dropped him to the edge of unconsciousness. At those moments he briefly forgot where he was and who was with him. Probably the best thing would have been to have turned back—or better not to have started at all in

12

this state—but he simply couldn't admit the thought that he might have anything seriously wrong with him. The war was bad enough without being ill. None of the partisans was ever ill enough to be relieved of his duties, especially not for something as trivial as a cold. Lots of them had coughs and colds, but in the forest a cold didn't count as an illness. And when the group commander had called his name back there at the campfire in the swamp, Sotnikov hadn't given his illness a thought. A moment later, when he discovered that the mission was to go out for supplies, he even felt pleased, because he'd been hungry for a long time, and there was a chance of sitting for an hour or two in the warmth and comfort of a proper house.

So much for warmth and comfort.

It had been a little easier in the forest, but here, out in the wind, he felt very ill, even afraid that he might fall, his head was spinning so much, and he was weaving form side to side with fatigue.

'How's it going?'

Rybak had stopped and turned round, and that simple question, which needed no answer, brought a touch of warmth to Sotnikov's heart. The thought that most troubled Sotnikov was that he might become a burden to his companion, although he knew that if it came to the worst he would find his own way out without becoming a burden to anyone, even to Rybak, who appeared to be the kind of person whom he could rely on. Since the time, not long back, when the two of them had crossed the main highway under covering fire from the rest of the group, they had somehow become fairly close, and they had stuck together through these last difficult days. That was probably why they had found themselves picked for this particular mission.

'We've only got to get through the valley, and then the village is just over the rise,' said Rybak encouragingly. 'We're quite close now.' He slowed down to let Sotnikov catch up.

They walked down the slope into the hollow. The snow was deeper here than on top of the hill, and their feet often crunched through the thin crust. By now the moon was behind them. The wind gusted erratically over the surface of the snow, whipping Sotnikov's short greatcoat about his freezing knees. Rybak looked closely at his companion.

'You know, I know nothing about you at all. What were you in the army—surely not a private?'

13

'Captain.'

'Infantry?'

'Artillery.'

'Oh, so you wouldn't have had much walking to do. Me, I was in the infantry, walked all the way.'

'Did you get far?' Sotnikov was thinking about his trek to the east. But Rybak took his meaning differently.

'Well just as far as you can see. I've come down from sergeant to private again. You a regular?'

'Not quite. I was teaching in a school until 1939.'

'Oh, went to college, did you?'

'Teachers training college. Two-year course.'

'I left school when I was thirteen. But even if . . .'

Rybak broke off as he plunged into the snow up to his knees. He swore quietly and altered course a little. They were just coming into the coppice, where there were willow and reeds and the snow was much softer and crumbly. It looked as if there was swamp underneath. Sotnikov stopped and stood uncertainly, trying to decide where to stop.

'Try to keep up with me. Walk in my footprints, it'll be easier for you,' Rybak called back from way up front, and moved determinedly off into the shrub.

Sotnikov staggered slightly, and didn't pick up Rybak's trail immediately, but soon he too had got into the undergrowth.

For some time they struggled through the shrub, along the side valley, crawled through clumps of frozen reeds which whispered despairingly around them, crossed the snow-choked brook, and came out on to a low-lying stretch of level ground, wading through the deep soft snow. Sotnikov was completely exhausted. He found it harder and harder to breathe, and felt he could barely make it to solid ground. Finally they left the shrub behind, and the ground began to rise steeply ahead of them. There was less snow lying now, but the climb made the going just as hard. Sotnikov was so tired that he felt totally detached from reality, and only a tremendous effort of will enabled him to stay on his feet and keep moving. His ears buzzed and rang—perhaps from the wind, perhaps from sheer exhaustion.

Halfway up the long slope it became quite unbearable. His legs began to give way. Fortunately there wasn't much snow here, and in places the wind had cleared it completely, revealing bald frost-

14

dusted patches of soil. Rybak had gone far ahead, probably so he could have a scout round when he got to the top of the hill. The village couldn't be far away. But before he got to the crest he stopped. It seemed to Sotnikov that he might have seen something, but from where he was it was hard to tell. The slope of the snow-covered hill stretched upwards towards the stars, where it seemed to dissolve and disappear in the night like a shadowy mirage. Behind him the grey misty plain extended into the distance, broken by the irregular outline of the thicket in the valley, and then further away, just barely visible from here, there was the dark mass of the forest they had left behind them. The forest was a long way back now, and all about them was the silent, bitter cold of the night. If anything were to happen, there was no hope of help from anywhere.

Rybak was still standing with his back to the wind when Sotnikov somehow or other staggered up to him. He had long since lost Rybak's trail, and had been letting his feet fall anywhere, not caring so long as he didn't fall. When he caught up, he suddenly realised that Rybak was standing on a road.

Neither of them spoke. They listened, gazed into the darkness, and then set off up the track, one on the right, one on the left. The track probably led into the village, so Sotnikov still had a chance of making it without falling. All around them stretched the shadowy spaces of night, the greyness of the open country, the snow, and the darkness with its multitude of tenuous, fleeting shadows. Nowhere was there any sign of light or movement. The earth lay silent, frozen, holding its breath.

'Quiet!' Rybak took one step and froze. The snow squeaked briefly under his boot and was silent again. Sotnikov stood motionless beside him. From the direction the track was taking them came the indistinct sound of a human voice. A fragment of a shout of some kind broke the silence and died away. Alarmed, they peered into the darkness. It looked as if the village was not far ahead, down in the valley below them. There was a vague stretch of something large and darker grey in the greyness of the night, although they couldn't make out anything in detail.

Standing motionless there on the road, they looked at each other for a moment, unable to make up their minds whether they had really heard a shout or whether they had imagined it. Around them the wind whistled through the coarse grass thrusting through the snow, and the frozen night was mute. Then, clearer this time, they heard the voice again, shouting an order maybe, or perhaps a curse, and then, removing any shadow of doubt, a shot rang out far away, and its echo rolled round the open country where they stood.

Rybak, apparently inferring something from all this, heaved a sigh of relief, and Sotnikov coughed suddenly, probably because he had been holding his breath so long.

For a few moments he could not control the cough, no matter how hard he tried, straining his ears to catch new sounds. But they needed no new sounds to know who had fired that shot; who else could it be but the Germans or their Russian henchmen, shooting in the country at this time of night? In other words, the way ahead was closed to them. They would have to turn back.

But there were no more shots, although the gusting wind twice brought them something like a voice—either conversation or a shout, it was so faint they couldn't make it out. After waiting a moment, Rybak spat into the snow.

'They're on the trail, the bastards! For the mighty Fatherland!'

They stood for a moment or two longer, listening to the sighing of the wind, worrying about what to do, where to turn next. As if he was hoping for some further development, Rybak went on gazing into the darkness where the track disappeared. Sotnikov just turned his back to the wind and shivered silently.

'No good shoving our noses in there.' Rybak shifted from side to side, his feet squeaking in the snow. 'Are you OK? How'd it be if we went down through the valley? There ought to be another village down there, if I remember right.'

'All right,' Sotnikov agreed curtly, his shoulders shuddering from the cold. He didn't care where they went—anywhere to get out of this stabbing wind. His emotions had become blunted into a kind of dream state, and his head was spinning again. He had to give his whole attention to not stumbling and falling.

They turned off the road and set off across the untrodden snow towards where the undergrowth showed up as a broad dark mass. At first the snow on the slope was a mere light covering, ankle-deep, but gradually it got deeper, particularly as they got down to the valley floor. Fortunately the swampy stretch was narrow. They were soon across it and turned to follow the line of the low brushwood without getting too close to it. Sotnikov had lost his sense of direction and relied absolutely on Rybak, who had scouted

16

round this area the previous autumn when the paths were clear and their group had been just beginning to muster its forces in the Gorely swamp. They had begun with minor sabotage on the road, and then gone on to bigger and better things—they had blown up a bridge at Islyanka and burned down a flax factory in the village; but once a senior German official had been killed, the occupiers really pulled themselves together. At the end of November three companies of the German-run Russian gendarmerie—the *politsai*—surrounded the Gorely swamp and launched a raid from which they had only just managed to escape into the Borkovskiy forest close by.

But at that time Sotnikov had been far away, without a thought in his head of partisans. He was engaged on his third attempt to penetrate the line of the front, and it had never occurred to him that he might leave the army. For twelve days he and a small artillery company worked their way from Shara up to Slonim. The company was all that was left of a once powerful artillery regiment. While the regiment were crossing the Berexina river almost all of them had been shot from ambush, sunk, or taken prisoner by the Germans.

Yes, they'd been good lads, his gunners, his scouts, spotters, signallers. All the year round he'd got top marks and praise from the high command for their training, their skill and markmanship in regimental and army manoeuvres.

But once the war got under way it all turned out differently. The battery only had a few brief seconds to set up, aim and fire, and the best results came from the men who settled down quickest and loaded fastest, those with the clearest heads who kept on coolly with their work at moments when their hands were trembling.

Rybak was striding determinedly ahead along the edge of a small wood. The snow here was not deep, and Sotnikov's clumsy, tattered felt boots, which he had recently acquired from the body of a local partisan, scuffed evenly over the broken surface of the snow. They were moving downwards with the wind now coming at them from the side, while the moon shone dimly and calmly from just over the horizon. The cold and the wind were always with them, and Sotnikov felt as if his guts had shrunk and shrivelled from his illness. It seemed as if he had never experienced such bitter cold as on this accursed night. Fatigue and the monotonous murmuring of the wind in the undergrowth filled his head with a humming confusion of random thoughts, disconnected fragments of sentences and conversations . . .

The worst thing of all for Sotnikov was that this was his first and last taste of front-line fighting, for which he had been preparing throughout his entire army service. The machinery of war waited obediently for his orders, the shells were ready, and at his side the crews were poised to show the enemy the firepower of their guns. Unfortunately this misbegotten battle demonstrated yet again the immutable but often ignored fact that an army derives not merely its strength, but also its weakness, from mastering the experience of previous wars. Probably what determines the character of war is not so much the usual run of events in a former conflict as the departures from the norm which led to victory or defeat. The pity of it was that Sotnikov realised this too late, when the lessons to be learnt from his brief front-line experience had already lost their usefulness, and all the might of his battery had been reduced to a heap of crumpled metal on the cobbled highway near Slonim.

All this seemed to him now like a terrible nightmare and, although he had had his share of horrifying experiences since, that first battle would never be erased from his memory.

... For four days the roaring column of the regiment had hauled itself along forest tracks and country roads to the west. Then it had turned south, but only managed a dozen kilometres before it was diverted north. The tractors deafened the neighbourhood with their implacable din, the water boiling in their overheated radiators, and sweat worked clear channels through the grime on the soldiers' faces. German planes swooped overhead from first light to dusk. Junkers incessantly sprayed the column with bombs. All the way everything was choked and clogged with sand and soil: there was the bitter smell of burnt-out vehicles. The column never halted, and had to skirt round the wrecks which littered the road. Soldiers with rifles fired sporadically from the gun-carriages, but their bullets made little difference. They were not even able to force the planes to rise above treetop height.

Sotnikov sat in the leading tractor, longing—as he might have longed for distraction, or for some great happiness—for the order to turn off this cursed road, disperse, and confront the enemy. Then, he thought, they would bring down on the Hun's head a weight of firepower he had never dreamt of. But there wasn't even an order to halt, the regiment kept on and on, while every two hours the ravaging Junkers and Heinkels, under whose attacks all this firepower was totally defenceless, dumped their bombloads.

18

And so they came to their last night of wandering along the roads of West Byelorussia.

The regiment was already a shadow of its former self. Several crews had been killed, and in his battery one gun had been blown to bits on the road by a near direct hit. True, three of his guns were still intact, apart from great gashes in their armour plating, their chassis twisted, and masses of shrapnel scars on their barrels and carriages. Oil flowed from the shattered crankcase of his second gun. The bodies of his four dead gunners lay on ammunition cases in a trailer, and the seven wounded men had been sent back to the rear. But theirs weren't the most sever losses—other batteries had suffered far worse. The regimental column had been cut to barely half its original length. Some guns had had to be left on the road. The damaged tractors could not haul them, and there were no tractors in reserve. They had spent almost the whole night moving east, and that was a bad sign. The adjutant, smoking cigarettes from Sotnikov's packet, hinted that they were being surrounded, and it really looked as if that might be happening. The soldiers had not slept for four days, although several, sitting on the gun-carriages, had managed to snatch a few moments just before dawn—the night was the quietest time, apart from the uncertainty of their position and the black mood which hung over the regiment. Before dawn they halted briefly in a village, and met a bunch of infantrymen moving in the opposite direction. A little way off, the night sky was lit by something burning after an incendiary attack—a railway station, someone said. No one told them anything—it was clear that the officers knew as little as the men—but everyone had reached the same conclusion for themselves—they were very close to the enemy. Soon the regimental commander, Major Prakhnevich, turned the column into a side-road lined with osiers. Now they were moving somewhere south. The night was more peaceful without the German planes, but the column was blind and deaf; nothing could be heard above the roar of the tractor engines, and you can't see much in the darkness of a summer night. Just before sunrise Sotnikov could hold out no longer. He had just dozed off in his seat when a thunderous explosion to the side tore him from his sleep. He was showered in earth and buffeted by the hot belch of the blast. He jumped from the tractor, which settled down hard on its right caterpillar track. And then it all began . . .

It was just getting light, and beyond the line of osiers the bright

19

blue of the sky met the grey of the oat-field. From somewhere forward, at the head of the column, tanks began to shoot them up. Sotnikov had barely got clear of his vehicle when a tractor from the third battery went up close by in a sheet of flame, and its howitzer plunged into a crater. Deafened, he ordered his battery to disperse to right and left, but it was far from easy to turn the big guns on the narrow road. The second outfit plunged over the ditch into the oats, and immediately two shells exploded on the tractor and the howitzer leapt sideways, leaving one wheel spinning in the air. The morning was lit up by vivid flames from the burning tractors, and the young trees disappeared in clouds of acrid smoke—the tanks were firing at the regiment along the road.

It was the worst that could possibly have happened—they were dying with their guns almost unused. Realising that he had a few meagre seconds left, Sotnikov and his crew somehow or other turned the one remaining workable howitzer in the road, and without securing the carriage managed to drag the cover from the barrel and load up a heavy shell. At first he couldn't see where the tanks were—the vehicles at the head of the column were in flames, the surviving crews were running down the line, and the smoke and the disabled tractors on the road made aiming acutely difficult. But half a minute later he saw through the trees the first German tank, which slowly crawled over the ditch, swung its turret and raked the column with rapid fire. Sotnikov thrust the gunner aside—the weapon was already ready to fire—and with trembling hands swung the massive barrel, finally picking up the dim shape of the advancing monster on the cross threads of his sights.

The explosion was like a clap of thunder. The howitzer recoiled violently, and the back-sight struck Sotnikov a painful blow on the cheek. The unsecured tail of the gun drew sparks from the cobbles, and one side of the carriage embedded itself deep in the side of the ditch, while the other remained firmly on the road. He still couldn't see anything through the cloud of dust his shot had raised, but he heard a shout of delight from the gunner, and realised that he must have scored a hit. He dived back to the sight and picked up the second tank moving along the road. He brought his barrel up against its grey turret—so close it seemed in the 'scope—and yelled 'Fire!' The loader had reacted quickly, and again the shot deafened him, but this time he managed to duck away from the back-sight. Through the smoke from the barrel he saw the tank which had been

20

standing there a second ago disintegrate like an eggshell, as a heavy interior explosion flung huge pieces of metal hurtling through the air. The heavy howitzer, designed for long-range fire from well behind the lines, had smashed the tank to fragments.

Suddenly the scent of victory was in their nostrils. They paid no more attention to their losses, to their dead and wounded, who lay streaming with blood on the cobbles, to the blaze which was devouring so many of their weapons, to the hail of bullets which streamed from the tanks. The few remaining guns took up an unequal battle with the tanks. . . . Meanwhile it grew lighter, and it was easier to aim. On the other side of the road smoke rose from some of the burning German tanks.

Sotnikov fired six more heavy shells, and blew two more tanks to atoms. But an intuition, sharpened by danger, warned him that their success was running out, that by fate or by chance he had exhausted the last few seconds which remained to him, and that one of the next few shells from the tanks would have his name on it. There could be no one left alive at the head of the column. The regimental commander had come staggering back and fallen on to the gun, blood pouring from him. Down in the ditch a few soldiers kept up rifle-fire, aiming at the driving slits of the tanks. Sotnikov's loader, Kogotkov, lay by the ammunition cases, his head pressed to the ground. There was no one else left. Sotnikov dashed on all fours towards the ammunition cases, but had still not reached them when a deafening explosion behind him flattened him on to the cobbles. A suffocating black cloud completely blocked his way for some seconds. Choking with soil and dust, he knew in a corner of his mind that he was still alive, and immediately, under a shower of humid, foul-smelling earth which was still descending from above, he dashed back to his gun. But the howitzer was tipped uselessly on its side by the edge of a crater, its barrel twisted awry by the force of the explosion, and there was a smell of burning rubber from the tyres. He realised that this was the end. He couldn't be sure whether he was wounded or not, he only knew that he was deaf. Explosions quite close to him seemed to have been sealed off behind a thick soundproof wall, and all other sounds had gone completely. His head was filled with a prolonged, painful ringing. Blood was flowing from his nose. He smeared it clumsily across his face and crawled from the road into the ditch. Opposite, beyond the trees, a tank, probably the one that had blown him up, waddled heavily along on

21

its tracks. The fresh morning breeze dispersed the heavy black smoke from the blazing tractor. There was a heavy acrid smell of TNT, and pale smoke rose from the smouldering battledress of the regimental commander, who had died slumped across the gun.

Shaken by the swiftness of destruction, Sotnikov gazed in bewilderment for a moment at the German tanks moving along on the other side of the road, at their numbers and the black and white crosses painted on their sides. Then someone grabbed him by the sleeve. He turned his head to see the smoke-grimed, blood-smeared face of a soldier who was shouting something and pointing down the line to the rear and at the soldiers dashing back along the ditch.

They leapt to their feet and, bent double, set off back through the choking smoke which hung over the road.

3

Rybak moved round a clump of the underbrush and stopped. Ahead on the slope of the hill the greying space of night dimly revealed the outline of the first buildings of the village. Rybak had forgotten how it looked from here. Once in the early autumn they had passed by on the road, but they hadn't gone into the village. But at the moment he hadn't time to think about that—the important thing was to work out whether there were any Germans here, or Russian *politsai*, so as not to walk straight into a trap.

He stood for a moment in the undergrowth, listening, but he could hear no suspicious sounds in the village. There were a few rustlings, muffled by night; a dog stretched itself lazily and yawned; the wind was still blowing persistently, naggingly, whistling through the frozen branches. There was a smell of smoke—someone's stove must still be alight. Meanwhile Sotnikov came up and stood beside him, peering into the darkness.

'Well?'

'Seems quiet enough,' said Rybak in a low voice. 'Let's go on a bit.'

It would have been quickest and easiest to go straight to the nearest house, which they could just make out, snow drifted right up to the windows, at the very end of the street. But there was always a grave risk attached to the last house in a village. Guards and sentries usually finish their patrols at the last house in the street, and that's where the *politsai* set up their ambushes. Rybak turned aside in the snow. They moved along a barbed-wire fence and crossed a little hollow, approaching the nearby buildings clustered at the end of the vegetable patches. They came to the communal threshing floor, and paused for a moment by the crumbling corner of a barn or granary with its roof full of holes. They listened again, and then Rybak peered round the corner and came out into the

23

open. From where he stood he could almost have reached out and touched a low-built, forlorn, tumbledown cottage with a narrow path trodden in the snow to a tiny outhouse. Rybak took two steps along the path, and immediately stepped off into the snow because of the noise his boots made. Sotnikov followed him, and they moved along the track towards the cottage.

They were still some way short of the outhouse when they heard the sound of someone chopping wood, apparently reluctantly and rather feebly. Rybak felt more cheerful. If people were chopping wood, that probably meant they wouldn't have to knock at windows and ask to be let in. They would be able to ask the woodcutter all they needed to know. Simultaneously it occurred to him that they might terrify whoever it was if they weren't careful—when the woodcutter saw strangers he might dash off and hide, and then there'd be all the trouble of trying to get him to come out of his cottage. So he moved round the corner of the shed as quietly as he could, stepped over a pile of branches lying on the floor, and emerged into the open.

In the dark grey shadows of the yard he could not at first make out the hunched female figure by the fence. When she heard footsteps, the woman cried out in alarm.

'Quiet, mother!' Rybak said in a low voice.

She stood in front of him in complete confusion, a short, elderly woman with a dirty kerchief bound tightly round her head. She seemed unable to utter a single word. Rybak glanced cautiously at the cottage door. In fact he was not greatly worried, as he had decided that the village was safe. The *politsai* would have stayed only as long as the home-brewed hooch lasted, and it was hardly likely that the Germans would be here themselves.

'Oh, dear God, how you frightened me. Oh, my God . . .'

'OK. You've crossed yourself enough. Are there many *politsai* in the village?'

'No, there aren't any. There was one, but they've just moved him off to the town. And there haven't been any others since.'

'Right.' Rybak walked round the yard and glanced round the corner. 'What's the village called?'

'Lyesiny.' The old woman was watching him closely, seemingly still frightened. Her axe was deeply embedded in the pine-log which she had been trying to split.

Rybak had already made his mind up that it would be no bad

24

thing to lie up here for a while. The approach to the village was good, and so were the ways out; the granary and the wood would be useful places to hide, if anything should happen.

'Who else is there at home?'

'I live alone, of course,' the woman replied, as if astonished by his lack of knowledge.

'And no one else?'

'No one. I live alone.' A note of complaint had come into her voice, but she kept her eyes on him, alarmed and expectant, as if she were trying to work out the purpose of this nocturnal visit. Rybak was not moved by her self-pitying, humble tone of voice. He was familiar with the ways of peasant women, and it was hard to move him to pity. At the moment he was more concerned with assessing the situation. He noticed the open doors of the shed, and glanced into the dense gloom of the interior, which was heavy with the smell of manure.

'Empty, is it?'

'It is indeed,' the woman confirmed miserably, still standing beside her chopping-block. 'They took everything.'

'Who are "they"?'

'Who do you think? Just because my son's in the Red Army. Just to show us who's boss.'

Rybak looked at the woman with a sudden flash of sympathy. If she could show bitterness, it meant that she wasn't lying, that she could be trusted. And he clicked his tongue impatiently as he realised that there was nothing to be had here—they couldn't take the last crumb from her, as the Germans had already done that. They'd have to look elsewhere.

Sotnikov, his head reeling, was waiting wearily, leaning against the wall. Rybak walked over to the woman.

'What's the matter? Can't you split that log?'

The old woman guessed that he was going to help her, and cheered up noticeably, dropping her air of defensive caution.

'No, curse it. I've been chopping at it, but I can't get through. I've been at it since evening, and I can't do a thing with it.'

'Let me.'

Rybak slung his rifle round his back and grabbed the smooth, dry handle of the axe with both hands. With a grunt he slammed the log against the chopping-block once, and again. His movements were neat, and he enjoyed the sensation of strength in his arms and the familiar skill he had known since childhood, when on winter evenings like this he had been sent to chop wood for the morning. He had never liked sawing, but he'd always been willing to chop; he always took pleasure in this difficult job with its feel of masculine prowess.

At the fourth blow the wood split, and the log fell into two halves. He chopped these into quarters.

'Oh, thank you, son. God give you health and strength.' The old woman thanked him without a hint of her former reticence.

'We need more than your thanks, my old dear. Have you got any food?'

'Food? What kind of food? There's some bread left. Not much. If you like, I could cook you some flour cakes.'

'That's no use to us! We need to take the stuff away with us. We could do with a cow or a sheep.'

'A beast! Can't think where you'll get one now . . .'

'Who lives there?' Rybak pointed over the garden, where he could see the snow-covered roof of the neighbouring building sticking up above the sharp, pointed stakes of the fence. It looked as if they had got the stove going there; there was a smell of food and cooking on the wind.

'Oh, that's Pyotr Kachan. He's the headman here now,' said the old woman.

'Is he now? The headman. D'you hear that?' Rybak turned to Sotnikov, who was still leaning patiently against the wall.

'Yes. The Germans made him headman.'

'Kind of a bastard, is he?'

'Oh, I wouldn't say that. He's one of our people. He comes from here.'

Rybak paused for a moment and then made his mind up.

'Right, let's go and see the headman. He's probably a bit better off than you are.'

They didn't bother going round by the path, but ducked under the rail of the fence, crossed the garden covered in ashes and potato peelings, and entered the headman's yard through a hole in his fence.

The yard was much tidier than the old woman's. There were signs everywhere of the master's hand. The yard had buildings on three sides—the cottage, the cattle shed, and a flimsy lean-to. By the porch there was a sled with wisps of hay lying in the bottom—a sure sign that the master was at home. A decent stack of firewood, sawn and chopped, was piled in the shed.

While they were crossing the garden, Rybak noticed a faint flicker of light through the frost-encrusted window, probably from a lamp. He stepped firmly up the creaking steps of the porch.

He did not knock. The outer door wasn't locked, and Rybak, born a peasant himself, had no difficulty with the latch. A quarter-turn of the handle, and the door swung open, creaking slightly. He moved through into the pitch-dark entrance passage, breathing in the half-forgotten smells of a peasant house which hung heavily on the air. He groped cautiously along the wall. First his fingers touched a frost-stiffened garment hanging from a nail, and then moved on to the door-frame. Feeling under the curtain which hung over the inner door, he easily found the latch, always the same in peasants' houses. It, too, was unlocked. He pulled it towards him and stepped over the high threshold, leaving the door-handle in Sotnikov's cold hand.

The lamp was standing on an upturned bowl in the middle of the table, and its flame flickered momentarily from the draught of cold air which came in with them. An elderly man with a close-trimmed beard, sitting at the table with a sheepskin coat slung round his shoulders, raised his grey head. An annoyed expression flickered across his broad face, oddly lit from below, but the irritation swiftly died away beneath his lowered grey brows.

'Good evening.' Rybak greeted him with restrained courtesy.

Of course, he could have approached a German collaborator without that kind of greeting, but Rybak didn't want to launch straight into a conversation which he knew he was not going to enjoy. The old man, however, did not reply. He didn't even move from the table. He merely looked at them without displaying any curiosity.

Behind them the cold was still creeping into the room. Sotnikov was clumsily rattling the door, trying in vain to get it shut. Rybak turned and closed it with an experienced shove. The old man finally straightened up from the table, but without altering the detached expression on his face, as if he hadn't guessed who these unbidden night visitors were.

'You're the headman here?' Rybak asked formally, walking clumsily over to the table. His ill-fitting boots, taken from the corpse of a dead German, were slippery with frost, and he moved

27

with exaggerated care. The old man sighed and, realising the kind of conversation that was to follow, closed the thick book he had been reading by the light of the lamp.

'That's right. I'm the headman,' he said in a voice which showed neither alarm nor servility. At that moment there was a rustle from the curtained-off area behind the stove, and a small, lean and very lively-looking woman emerged, adjusting her headscarf. Clearly this was the headman's wife. Rybak unslung his rifle and lowered the butt to the floor.

'Have you guessed who we are?'

'I'm not blind. But if you've come for vodka, you're wasting your time. They've taken everything.'

Rybak looked significantly at Sotnikov. The old fool. Surely he didn't take them for members of the *politsai*? Well, perhaps it's better if he does, he thought. Rybak turned back to the old man with his former expression of cool amiability.

'Never mind, we'll get by without vodka.'

The headman didn't reply, as if he were thinking something over. He moved the bowl with the lamp closer to the edge of the table, where it cast more light on the floor.

'If it's like that then, sit down.'

'Yes, sit down, sit down, lads,' chirped the headman's wife, delighted at the invitation. She dragged the bench from the table over to the stove, which had clearly been banked up with wood for the night. 'You'll be warmer here, you must be frozen. What a frost tonight!'

'Yes, we could sit a while,' agreed Rybak, although he didn't sit down himself. He nudged Sotnikov. 'Sit down, get yourself warm.'

Sotnikov didn't need to be persuaded. He immediately lowered himself on to the bench and propped his back against the whitewashed side of the stove. He kept his rifle in his hands, as if he were leaning on it, and didn't even take off his forage cap, leaving it pulled down low over his frost-reddened ears. Rybak was getting warmer. He unfastened the top buttons of his sheepskin coat and pushed his hat on to the back of his head. The headman was still sitting at the table with the same unconcerned expression on his face, while his wife, her arms folded across her stomach, followed every movement closely and anxiously. She's afraid, Rybak thought. Before he sat down he went through his partisan routine of checking out the cottage. He looked casually behind the stove and

28

went over to a red plywood cupboard which divided off the corner which housed the bed. The wife moved respectfully to one side to let him pass.

'There's no one there, lads.'

'There's just you living here?'

'Just us. That's the way it turned out,' the woman said sadly. And then, suddenly, not so much an offer as a question: 'Perhaps you'll have something to eat? You must be hungry? Of course you are, out in the frost with no food . . .'

Rybak smiled faintly and rubbed his frozen hands together contentedly.

'Well, perhaps we will eat. What d'you think?' He turned to Sotnikov in feigned indecision. 'It'd set us up, seeing Madam headman is offering . . .'

'Good. I'll get something.' The woman beamed. 'The cabbage is probably still warm. And I could bake some rolls . . .'

'There's no need to bake. There isn't time.' Rybak sounded decisive. He looked out of the corner of his eye at the headman, who was still sitting motionless in the corner, his elbows propped on the table. Above his head there were three old ikons, their embroidered curtains drawn aside. Rybak moved heavily over to the wall between the windows and stood in front of a glazed frame which housed a number of photographs. He consciously avoided looking at the headman, as he felt that he himself was being covertly watched all the time.

'So, you work for the Germans?'

'I've got to,' sighed the headman. 'What else can you do?'

'Do they pay well?'

The old man could hardly have missed the open sneer in the question, but he answered quietly and with dignity:

'I haven't asked and I don't want to know. I'll get by with what I've got.'

Well, well, Rybak thought to himself. A man of principle.

The birchwood frame on the wall housed half a dozen photographs, in the middle of which Rybak spotted one of a young lad with a faint resemblance to the old man, wearing battledress with artillery badges and three decorations. There was something quiet and obedient in his look, but at the same time he gave the impression of youthful naive self-confidence.

'Who's that? Your son, is it?'

29

'Yes, that's our son, our Tolik,' the wife replied tenderly, looking at the picture over Rybak's shoulder.

'Where is he now? Not in the *politsai*, by any chance?'

The headman raised his wrinkled face.

'How would we know? He was at the front . . .'

'Oh God, he went off in thirty-nine, and the way things turned out, we haven't had sight nor sound of him since last summer. If only we knew whether he is still alive, or buried long since . . .' said the headman's wife, as she put two soup bowls on the table.

'I see,' said Rybak, showing no reaction to the old woman's dismal lament. When she had finished, he turned sharply on the headman.

'You have disgraced your son.'

'He has indeed. That's what I tell him night and day,' the old woman broke in from over by the stove. 'He's disgraced our son and all of us.'

This was a little unexpected, especially as the headman's wife spoke with what sounded like genuine pain in her voice. The headman, however, didn't react to her words, just sat motionless with his head lowered. Rybak suddenly thought that the old man was probably not quite all there. But the notion had only just struck him when the old man's scowling face scowled even more.

'That's enough. It's none of your business.'

The old man swung his reproachful eyes on Rybak.

'And hasn't he disgraced me? Didn't he surrender to the Germans?'

'That's just the way it happened. It wasn't his fault.'

'Whose was it then? Mine, perhaps?' The old man spoke severely, without a trace of shame or fear, and thumped the table emphatically. 'It was *your* fault.'

'We-ell,' said Rybak indecisively, not wanting to continue this unpleasant and for him rather complicated conversation, which, as he well knew, could produce no conclusion.

The woman unfolded a small tablecloth, which covered half the table, and set down a bowl of cabbage soup, whose meaty smell drowned every thought in Rybak's mind save his sharpening hunger. Rybak had no respect for this man, and no interest in the considerations which had made him accept the post of headman—the fact that he had undertaken to serve the Germans was sufficient for him. But now he was ravenously hungry, and he decided to

30

postpone for the moment any further clarification of the relationship between the old man and the Germans.

'Come on, sit down and get something inside you,' said the old woman with a kindly welcome.

Rybak, his hat still on the back of his head, slid behind the table.

'Come on, let's get on with eating,' he said to Sotnikov, who wearily turned his head away.

'You eat. I don't want anything.'

Rybak looked closely at his comrade, who was hunched, coughing, on the bench. Occasionally he shivered as well, as if he had a fever. The woman, who clearly had not noticed Sotnikov's condition, was astonished.

'Why won't you eat? Don't you like cabbage soup? Can I get you something else?'

'No, thank you. I don't need anything,' said Sotnikov firmly, pulling his thin wrists into his sleeves to get a bit of warmth into them.

The headman's wife was now genuinely disturbed.

'Oh, dear. Have I done something wrong? Please forgive me . . .'

Rybak made himself comfortable on the broad bench at the table, gripped his rifle between his knees, and didn't notice the total silence which reigned while he drained the bowl. The headman sat in his corner with the same grim expression on his face, while his wife hovered near the table waiting for an opportunity to serve her guest.

'Right. I'll take a little bread. That'll do for his share,' said Rybak, nodding in Sotnikov's direction.

'Do take some, take what you want, lads.'

The headman, it seemed, was silently waiting for something—a word, perhaps, or the start of the serious business of the evening. His big knotted hands lay calmly on the black binding of the book he had been reading. Rybak thrust the last piece of bread into the front of his coat, and said disapprovingly:

'Read books, do you?'

'So what? Reading never hurt anyone.'

'Is it Soviet or German?'

'The Bible.'

'Well, well. It's the first time I've ever seen a Bible.'

Rybak moved round the table and picked up the book curiously, and opened it. But then he felt that there was no call to do that—to reveal his interest in this strange book, a book which might even have been printed in Germany.

'That's a pity. Wouldn't do you any harm to read it,' the old man muttered.

Rybak slammed the Bible firmly shut.

'That's nothing to do with you. It's not your job to teach me anything. You serve the Germans, so you're our enemy,' Rybak said, feeling some satisfaction that he had been able to avoid the need to show any gratitude for the food, and in order to get on to a level of conversation more appropriate to the situation in hand. He came out from behind the table into the centre of the room, adjusting his belt, which was now a little too tight. This new turn in their relationship gave him a chance of getting down to brass tacks, although more preparation was still needed for the change of subject.

'You are an enemy. And you know how we deal with enemies.'

'It depends whose enemy I am,' the old man responded quietly but firmly, as if he was still not aware of the full gravity of his situation.

'Our enemy. Russia's enemy.'

'I am no enemy to my own people.'

The headman's stubborn refusal to agree was beginning to irritate Rybak. It was a bit much to have to prove to this quisling why, whether he liked it or not, he was an enemy of Soviet power. Rybak had no wish for that kind of argument with him, and asked him with an ill-concealed sneer:

'Did they use force to make you take the job on, then? Against your will?'

'No, why should they use force?' said the headman.

'In other words, you took it on of your own accord?'

'You could say so. Sort of.'

That's cleared that up, then, thought Rybak. No need to go any further into it. His distaste for the man was growing stronger; he was regretting the time wasted on a useless conversation, when everything had been clear from the very beginning.

'Right, let's go,' he ordered harshly.

Wringing her hands, the headman's wife flung herself at Rybak.

'Oh, my son, where are you taking him? There's no need, forgive the old fool. He's an old man, and he's made a fool of himself in his old age . . .'

But the headman did not force Rybak to repeat the order, and with admirable self-control rose from the table and thrust his arms into the sleeves of his sheepskin. He was completely grey-haired and, despite his age, tall and broad-shouldered. When he rose he filled the entire ikon corner.

'Shut up!' he ordered his wife.

Apparently she was accustomed to obey. She burst into tears and slipped behind the curtain. The headman eased himself out from behind the table cautiously, as if he were afraid of breaking something.

'Right then. Do what you want. Beat me up. If it's not you, then it'll be the others. They've already stood me against a wall and shot at me.' He nodded briefly at the wall.

Rybak found himself following the old man's nod. Surely enough, there were holes in the white wall by the window which looked like marks of bullets.

'Who shot at you?'

'People like you. They wanted vodka.'

Rybak shuddered. He didn't like the comparison. He still reckoned that his intentions were justified, but the thought that people he despised had apparently had the same intentions gave him pause for thought. And he could not believe that the headman was tricking him—people don't lie in that tone of voice. The headman's wife, sobbing quietly, peered out from behind the curtain. Sotnikov was hunched on the bench, coughing; he had not contributed a single word to the conversation with the old man. Clearly, he was not himself.

'Right. Do you have a cow?'

'Yes. Until now,' the old man replied, without showing any interest in the new turn the conversation had taken. The old woman stopped weeping and quietened down, listening. Rybak thought for a moment. The idea of driving a cow back into the forest was attractive, but it would be a very long way, and they might not make it back by the morning.

'Let's go then.' He slung his rifle on his shoulder. The headman obediently put on a hat he took from a nail, and silently opened the door. Rybak followed him out, telling Sotnikov as he left, 'You wait here.'

4

As soon as the door had closed behind them, the old woman rushed to the threshold.

'Oh, my God! Where's he taking him? What's he done? Oh, my God!'

'Get back,' Sotnikov managed to croak out and, without rising from the bench, stretched out a leg to block her way to the door. The woman stopped, frightened, and retreated to the centre of the room. Sometimes she sobbed and sometimes fell silent, straining to hear what was going on outside. The sense of Rybak's conversation with the old man had largely passed Sotnikov by, but what had penetrated to his fever-clouded mind had tended to suggest that Rybak was going to shoot the headman.

But time passed, and no shot came. The woman covered her mouth with a corner of her headscarf and moaned and wailed, while Sotnikov sat on the bench watching in case she slipped out into the yard and raised the alarm. He felt very bad. His cough was bothering him, his head ached violently and, although he was sitting next to the hot stove, waves of cold swept over him.

'Let me go out, son! Let me go and see what they're . . .'

'There's nothing to see.'

The woman wandered blindly around in the shadows of the room, wailing all the time, doubtless in an attempt to make him pity her and let her out. But that wouldn't do her any good, he wouldn't give in to her weeping and moaning. He well remembered how last summer he had almost lost his life because he had trusted just such an old woman too much. That one, too, had been simple and kindly-faced, with a white headscarf. When he had come out of the forest, he had noticed her straight away standing among the beets in her garden, and had thought she'd be able to show him how to get on to the track through the Chorniye Vygory swamp, which only had one path across it, starting from that village.

He had come out of the damp undergrowth and made his way through a patch of high flax unseen by anyone, and got quite close to her, as she bent over the beds, hoeing between the rows. To this day he could clearly remember her dark skirt, tucked up to show her white sun-starved calves, and a sort of worn short jacket and a shawl round her shoulders. She was tending her beets and hadn't noticed him. He greeted her quietly, and to his surprise she was not alarmed, just looked steadily at him, listening to, but apparently not understanding, his simple question.

Then she explained it all very clearly—how to get on to the path, how to get across the plank bridge, what side to pass by the clump of fir trees so as not to get into the swamp. He thanked her and was about to go on, when she looked round and said, 'Wait a moment, you must be hungry.' She gathered the beets into her skirt and led the way to the house. What a fool he'd been to agree. But he was as hungry as a wolf in spring, and obediently followed her in the happy anticipation of an enormous country breakfast.

While they walked, she had spoken kindly to him, called him 'son', and twice even, he recalled, 'my dear'. He was unshaven, as now, unwashed, soaked to the knees from the dew, and altogether in a pretty miserable state. He couldn't talk the local dialect or hide the fact that he was just out of the army—it must have been plain to anyone who he was and where he came from. He had no weapon of any kind—only the previous day he'd just managed to avoid death by a miracle when there seemed to be no hope of escape . . .

All this time the headman's wife kept up her moaning, wandering about the cottage and weeping.

'Son, why are you doing this to us? He'll shoot him!'

'You should have thought of that before,' said Sotnikov coldly, trying to hear what was going on outside.

'Oh lad, if I've told him once I've told him a hundred times, I've begged and begged! Why did he have to take this evil thing on? There were people who were younger. But the decent ones wouldn't do it, and people were afraid of the others.'

'Aren't they afraid of him?'

'Of Pyotr? Oh, everybody round here knows him, we've lived here all our lives. We're related to half the village. And he tries to behave decently to everyone.'

'It's a funny way of behaving decently.'

'Well, perhaps not quite that. Perhaps you're right, son—you can't be decent to everyone. He's obliged to do some unpleasant things. He has to get people to give bread or hand over clothes, and they make him get people out on the road to clear the snow. He has to get people where he can, and send his own people out to work.'

'Well, what did you expect? They're occupiers, they're here to steal.'

'And they do steal. They came with trucks and took our pigs away. We had a calf and they took that. They say, "You have a son in the Red Army. You must purge your guilt towards Germany." I wish their Germany would all catch fire and burn up.'

Curse as much as you like, but I don't believe you really, thought Sotnikov sleepily, leaving his outstretched leg where it was, blocking the door. That other woman, last summer, had said something similar about Germany while she was getting his food ready and cutting the bread. Several times she had dashed off into the passage, for dripping and a jug of milk, and he had sat on the bench at the table, his mouth watering, waiting like an idiot for his food. True, there were moments when he thought he heard voices outside—someone calling quietly, and then a quick whispered exchange, but he recognised the sleepy voice of a child and didn't worry about it. The woman came back into the room, calm and kindly, poured him a mug of milk and spread the dripping; he could remember how moved he had been by her kindness. He wolfed his bread and dripping, washed it down with the milk, and that would probably have been the last of him if some instinctive, unreasoning fear had not suddenly caused him to glance out of the flower-framed window. What he saw threw him into momentary confusion. Two men were walking down the street carrying rifles, the white armbands of the *politsai* round their sleeves. Alongside them, explaining something, ran a small child of about eight.

Unfortunately, for a moment he lost the power of speech and could find nothing to say to that kindly old woman. He just pushed her away from the door and dashed madly out into the garden and over the fence at full speed into the valley. Behind him there were shots, shouts and curses. Then when he was lying up in the valley, among the other voices he could make out the voice of his benefactress, but quite changed now—a loud-tongued virago, pointing out to the militia where he had hidden in the undergrowth.

And now here was this one with her 'son' and 'lad' . . .

The headman's wife calmed down a little since she could hear nothing terrible happening outside, and sat down on the end of the bench in front of him.

'Son, it's not true that he did it of his own free will. All the men from round here asked him to take it on. He really didn't want to. And then a paper came from the town—all the headmen had to go for a meeting. Here in Lyesiny there wasn't a headman. So all the men said, "Go on, Pyotr, you've been a prisoner"—and that's the truth, he was a prisoner at Nikolaevo for two years, and he worked for a German there. They said, "You know their ways, you stick it out a couple of months until our own people come back. If you don't, they'll make us have Budila, and that'll mean trouble." Budila's from Lyesiny, too, and he's a bad man. Before the war he was some kind of boss, he used to go round from village to village—everyone was afraid of him even then. And now he's gone and got himself a job in the *politsai*—he's like a pig in clover.'

'He'll live to see a bullet coming for him!'

'I hope so. No one'd weep for him, save the Devil . . . so Pyotr, the old fool, let himself be talked into it and went to the town—to his own grief and sorrow. You can't really think he wants to be the Germans' whipping boy? Every blessed day they come here and threaten him, they shout at him, they even stick a gun to his forehead, they scream for vodka and everything. Still, he'll live through it, if God wills.'

Sotnikov sat toasting himself by the stove, and, stretching painfully, tried to keep himself from falling asleep. His cough helped him stay awake: for a moment or two it would stop, and then a fit would seize him so fiercely that it seemed to wrench at his brain. The old woman's complaints flowed over him, sometimes penetrating, sometimes not—he had no wish to answer her. He could feel no sympathy for a man who had agreed to serve the Germans and who went on doing so, no matter how unwilling or inefficiently. The fact that the old man might have had some defensible reasons didn't impress Sotnikov, who knew the value of that kind of justification. In the cruel battle with fascism there was no room to pay attention to even the most apparently valid reasons—victory could only be won despite all those reasons. He had understood that since his very first battle, and had always held to that conviction, which had in its turn helped him to steer a firm course through all the vicissitudes of the war.

37

Afraid that he might fall asleep, Sotnikov tried to stand up, but the warmth of the cottage had so affected him that he all but stumbled and fell against the wall. The woman, startled, supported him somehow or other, and he managed to pick his rifle up from the floor.

'Oh, hell!'

'Son, what is it? What's the matter? You're ill. God have mercy! You're in a fever. You ought to lie down. And there's that awful wheezing in your chest. Wait a minute. Sit down and I'll just make you a drink from some herbs . . .'

Eager to help, she rushed into the space behind the stove and rummaged about in there. He probably was in a really bad way if the old woman was so worried about him, but he didn't want the headman's wife's potions.

'Don't worry. I don't want anything.'

In fact he had no wish to eat or drink. He wanted nothing but warmth and quiet.

'What d'you mean you don't want anything, son? You're ill, can't you see? I noticed it long ago. If you haven't got much time now, I'll give you some dried raspberries, you might be able to boil them up and make yourself a drink. And here's the herbal potion . . .'

'I want nothing.'

She thrust something at him from a little bag which she had taken from the top of the stove, but he refused it. He had no kindly thoughts towards this woman, and he could not agree to accept her sympathy and help. But at that moment someone walked into the passage and he heard Rybak's voice. The headman looked into the room.

'Go on out, your friend's calling you.'

He got up, his head swimming, staggering from weakness, and went into the cold dark passage. Through the open door to the snow-covered yard he saw Rybak, a dark-coloured sheep lying at his feet in the snow. He was preparing to lift it on to his shoulders.

'OK. Go indoors,' said Rybak to the old man, without the former scorn in his voice. 'And close the door, there's nothing out here to look at.'

It looked as if the headman had something to say, but, apparently changing his mind, he turned back into the house. He shut the outer door firmly behind him, and then they heard the

38

inner door close.

'Are you letting him go, then?' Sotnikov asked reproachfully, when they were left alone together in the yard.

'Oh, to hell with him.'

Rybak heaved the sheep on to his shoulder with one strong movement, and marched off round the corner of the shed, from where he set off across the unbroken snow towards the barn whose slanting walls could be seen nearby in the snow. Sotnikov hauled himself along behind.

5

They walked in silence back the way they had come—past the threshing floor, by the barbed-wire fence, and came out on to the shrub-covered slope. The village was still quiet, no glimmer of light came from the windows. The snow-covered roofs, walls, fences and trees slumbered grey in the darkness. Rybak strode off ahead with the sheep over his shoulders, its white-marked head jolting limply in the small of his back. It was probably well after midnight by now and the moon had climbed high into the sky and was shining cold and tranquil, surrounded by a bright misty halo. The stars sparkled more brightly than they had earlier, and the snow squeaked louder underfoot—the frost was biting at its hardest. Rybak thought regretfully about the time they had wasted in the old man's house—but at least they hadn't come away empty-handed. Of course one sheep wouldn't go far among seventeen men, but there would be a hunk of meat for everyone. They had something to show for their long trek—all they had to do now was to make it home before dawn.

Despite the weight of the sheep Rybak stepped out briskly, not too worried about where he set his feet on the now familiar track across open country. If it hadn't been for Sotnikov, who couldn't be left on his own, he could have got a long way by now. It was the first time that night that Rybak had felt the slightest prickling of irritation with his companion, but he suppressed it; nothing could be done about it; after all, it wasn't Sotnikov's fault. Still, he might have got hold of some warmer clothes from somewhere, and then he mightn't have got ill, and then he could have helped to carry the sheep. At first the beast had seemed quite light, but it gradually developed into quite a load, weighing heavier and heavier on his shoulders and forcing his head lower, which made it harder to follow the trail ahead. Rybak began to shift the load from shoulder to shoulder—while it was on one, it gave the other a chance for a breather, and it made the going easier

As he walked he grew comfortably warm in his good black sheepskin coat, which was almost new. It had done good service in this freezing winter. If it hadn't been for the coat he might have fallen by the wayside as well. And for the fact that he was fit and warm and that even in a bivouac in the snow he could still feel comfortable in it, he had to thank old Uncle Akhrem, who hadn't merely sympathised, but had handed the coat over. It was true that Akhrem had his own reasons for being so generous, the chief of which, of course, was Zosya, whose heart, he knew for a fact, had really warmed to him. He was an enviable catch, but a short-lived one because of the war.

But what if there hadn't been a war? In that case, what chance would there have been of his meeting Zosya? It would probably never have happened. Sergeant Rybak of the rifle brigade would never have landed up in Korchevka, their tiny isolated village deep in the forest. He would probably have never got closer to it than to have passed by it on the main road during the autumn manoeuvres. But, as it turned out, he had to lie up there with a wounded foot wrapped in a dirty, bloodstained shirt, and to ask for shelter in the cottage. He was afraid that the next day the Germans would arrive and sure as death pick him up if he stayed on the road. And he was right. At dawn they had roared in on motorcycles and had surrounded the corpse-strewn battlefield, while he was carefully hidden under a pile of peapods in the barn.

Akhrem and Zosya kept watch over him day and night—protected him, refused to betray him. And then . . . then everything quietened down again, the new German masters took control, and he couldn't even hear artillery fire at night. It was very gloomy. It seemed that everything he had lived and fought for had been destroyed for ever. It was a very bad time for him, and the only consolation of his depressing life in the village was kindly, plump Zosya. And even that didn't last long.

His health never let him down, there was plenty of milk and *smetana*, the wound in his foot cleared up within a month to the point where he could only just feel it as he walked. He began to spend more and more time thinking about how to get away, particularly when he heard that after their victories of the summer the Germans had got bogged down outside Moscow. No matter how

41

much they trumpeted their forecast that the capital would fall any day, Rybak thought that it might hold out. He oughtn't to be in Korchevka but in Moscow, using his strength to defend the capital.

Then other Red Army men began to appear, men who had been cut off like him, some of them recovering from wounds, some of them just loafing around the huts of the village, shattered by the first shock of the defeat. They began to gather, make plans, and produce hidden weapons. They decided they had to get away into the forest, that they'd loitered long enough round kitchen cupboards with the kind-hearted girls, the unspoken for, un-betrothed women of the village. And so they went.

His departure from Korchevka was not a pleasant occasion. True, he didn't try, as some of the others did, to deceive, or worse, to disappear without saying a word. He explained the way things were, and to his surprise they understood, didn't take offence, and didn't try to persuade him to stay. Zosya burst into tears of course, but Akhrem said, 'If you must go, you must. It's a military matter.' He and Aunt Ganulya gathered him in their arms as if he were the son they had never had. Rybak promised to let them know what happened to him, and to come to see them if he got the chance. Indeed once, towards the end of the autumn, he did get to see them, but after that the village always seemed to be a long way off and, what was more important, he didn't really want to return. He must have outgrown it. Or maybe it wasn't one of those affairs that last a long time—it had just sparked up, flared for a moment, and then died down. He didn't regret it, and was quite content with the part he had played—he hadn't deceived anyone, he hadn't lied, he had behaved openly and honestly. Let people judge as they will, his conscience was almost clear about Zosya.

He didn't like hurting people—he hated to cause pain whether by accident or on purpose—and he couldn't stand being disliked. It's true that in the army it was often difficult to avoid it—it used to happen, and he had to impose punishments, but he always tried to make things look decent, just for the sake of good order and military discipline. Now Sotnikov, a hard man, and exhausted by his fever, was reproaching him for not having punished the headman and letting him go, but Rybak hated punishing people—the hell with him, let him live. Of course, you couldn't collaborate with the enemy, but this Pyotr had seemed a very peaceful character, a familiar peasant type. Well, if he was a traitor, let someone else

42

punish him. While that unpleasant conversation had been going on in the cottage, Rybak had wanted to teach the headman a lesson, but afterwards, when they were dealing with the sheep, the feeling had gradually disappeared. The shed had had an everyday, peaceful smell of hay, dung and livestock. The three sheep had dashed wildly from corner to corner. Pyotr had made a grab at one with a white mark on its face, and then Rybak had caught it skilfully by the neck and felt for a moment the half-forgotten joy of the chase. While he held the beast and the headman cut its throat, and the sheep threshed about the straw, which was soaked with steaming blood, his veins were filled with some of the half-fearful joy he had felt as a boy when, just before the winter, his father had killed one or two sheep in the same way, and he, in his teens already, had helped him. Everything had been just the same—the smells of the byre, the way the sheep leaped about in terror, and the sharp, steaming reek of the blood on the frosty air.

Rybak had turned away from the shrub and struck out across open ground which extended a great deal further than he had expected. They must have been walking over it for the best part of an hour already. Rybak couldn't be absolutely certain, but he felt that somewhere along the way they were going they should come across a road, the one they had briefly followed on their way here, and that at that point they should begin the descent towards the brook. But a long time went by, during which they must have covered around two kilometres, and there was still no sign of a road. He began to worry that they might have crossed it already without noticing. If they had, they could easily lose their sense of direction and turn left down into the valley far later than they should. It was a pity that he was so unfamiliar with the area, and a pity, too, that he hadn't consulted the local partisans in the forest. He hadn't foreseen, though, that they would have to go so far afield.

Rybak stopped to wait for Sotnikov, who was wearily dragging himself along behind in the darkenss. A thick cloud drifted across the face of the moon. The night grew darker, and it was almost impossible to make out anything at any distance. Rybak flung the sheep down in the snow, propped his rifle against its flank and stretched his weary shoulders in relief. A moment later Sotnikov stumbled up.

'How are you doing? OK?'

'Well, I'm afraid you're going to have to manage somehow. I'm in no state to help today.'

'It's all right. I'll get by.' Rybak tried to shake off his own fatigue, and changed the subject. 'Does it look to you as if we're going the right way?'

Sotnikov gazed into the night, breathing heavily.

'It looks like the right way. The forest's over there.'

'What about the road?'

'The road must be around somewhere. If we haven't passed the turning already.'

They stood silently peering into the snow and the dark. At that moment, there was a loud gust of wind, on which their tensed ears caught a whisper of a distant, indefinite sound. The next instant they both recognised the far-off drumming of hooves. They turned to face into the wind, and didn't so much see as sense a barely visible flicker of movement in the darkness. At first Rybak thought that they were being followed, but then he realised that the movement was not following them but had cut across their tracks, probably travelling along the road they must have missed. He felt his heartbeat quicken, and slung his rifle back on to his shoulder. His instinct told him that someone was riding past them some way off, but he couldn't decide whether they would remain undiscovered. He bent down and heaved the shaggy body of the sheep back on to his shoulders. The ground ran to a crest. They had to get over the rise as quickly as they could, and then there was a good chance that they wouldn't be spotted.

'Come on, quick. Move!' he whispered urgently to Sotnikov, and broke into a run.

His legs immediately felt lighter, and his body, as it always did in moments of danger, acquired a reserve of strength and energy. Then suddenly, not five paces from where he was standing, he saw the road—its ruts cutting diagonally across the path they were following. This must be the road whoever it was was riding along. He looked back down the track and made out some dim, moving shapes. He could hear a faint jingling of harness—a sleigh was approaching. For a moment Rybak was confused, but then he dashed across the road, which had turned up as unexpectedly and awkwardly as a minefield, and knew immediately that that was a mistake. It would probably have been better to have gone back, keeping on the side of the road they were on, but it was too late to think about that now. He ran up to the crest, his boots breaking through the snow-crust, and waited, his heart sinking, for someone to challenge them.

Before he got to the top, where the slope began to run downwards into the valley, he looked back again. Now he could see the sleighs clearly, two of them, the second right on the tail of the first. But he could no longer make out the horsemen in the dark, and there were no more shouts. He began to allow himself a flicker of hope that the people in the sleighs might be peasants. If they didn't shout they probably were peasants who'd been delayed somewhere and were on their way back to their village, in which case there would be nothing to worry about. Relieved by this unexpected thought, he breathed more easily and, running on, turned to look back at Sotnikov, who, as luck would have it, was staggering close by, looking as if he were in no state to make the effort of running the hundred paces to the top of the hill.

Then a harsh, threatening shout shattered the silence of the night.

'Hey! Halt there!'

The hell with your halt! thought Rybak, and hurled himself forward with renewed energy. He was very close to the top, and it looked to him as if the descent into the valley started just there—that's where they should be making for. But at that moment the sleighs drew up, and several voices began bawling after them.

'Halt! Halt or we fire! Halt!'

We've had it! The worst thought of all flashed into Rybak's mind. Now everything was simple and painfully familiar. He ran wearily along the ridge, knowing in his agony that the main thing now was to get as far as possible. The others probably wouldn't be able to catch up on horseback, and if they felt like shooting, good luck to them—the odds would be against them in the dark. But he didn't drop the sheep lying awkwardly across his shoulders—he kept lugging it along, as if he couldn't bear to abandon the faint hope that they might somehow or other still get back.

Soon he was over the crest and plunging down the other side. His legs carried him at such a speed that he was afraid he might fall with his load. The butt of the German rifle slung over his shoulder banged his hip painfully, and his cartridges jangled together in his pockets. He saw a dark mass ahead, a thicket of trees, probably, and he altered course towards it. There hadn't been any shouting from behind for some moments, and no shots at all yet. It looked as if he and Sotnikov might have got out of sight of their pursuers.

But when he got to the bottom of the hill, the snow became deeper. A new worry struck Rybak, and he looked back. Sotnikov had fallen so far behind that he might be in danger of being taken alive. He didn't even seem to be hurrying now, he wasn't running, just dragging himself along in the snow and darkness. The worst thing was that there was nothing Rybak could do to help him. All he could do was go on forging ahead, dragging his comrade in his wake by sheer example and will-power. He had to get to the thicket.

'Halt, you damned bandits!' Threatening, cursing shouts rang out behind them again.

So they were catching up on them. Without looking back—the sheep made it rather difficult to do so—Rybak realised that their pursuers must be on the crest, and could probably see them. Their situation was now critical, especially for Sotnikov, who still had a long way to go to reach the thicket. But what could he do . . .? In moments of extreme danger, a man thinks of himself first, makes as sure as he can of his own safety. And that went for Rybak, whose legs had saved his life more than once already during the war.

It turned out that the thicket was a good deal further off than it had looked. Rybak had only got half-way to it when shots barked out behind him. But the shooting wasn't too sharp, as he could tell from the whine of a bullet which whipped past far over his head. They were aiming miles too high. He forced himself to go forward beneath the bullets to the thicket.

It looked as if he had reached the swampy bottom of the valley. Naked alder saplings thrust up through the level snow and there were soft tussocks of swamp grass lying beneath the wet surface. Rybak fell at the very edge of the thicket and dropped the sheep from his shoulders. He should have gone on running, but he simply didn't have the strength. There was still firing behind him, and he realised that Sotnikov was holding them off. At first that pleased Rybak—he'd got away, he could easily confuse his tracks in the thicket and go. But first he had to look back. With his rifle in his hand he rose cautiously to his knees and saw Sotnikov a long way off, high up below the crest of the hill. He seemed to be moving very slowly, but in the grey darkness of the night it was impossible to make out which way he was going or if indeed he was actually moving at all. After three or four shots from the top of the hill, there was one from closer at hand, and Rybak recognised the

46

unmistakable sound of Sotnikov's rifle. In their situation Rybak couldn't see the slightest point in beginning to shoot it out with the Russian *politsai*. Probably their best course would have been to make a break for it—the thicket would have given them a good chance of shaking off their pursuers. But Sotnikov seemed not to understand that, it looked rather as if he had lain down and wasn't even moving. If it hadn't been for the fact that he was firing occasionally he could have been taken for dead.

But perhaps he was wounded.

The thought threw Rybak into even deeper confusion, but there was nothing he could do to help Sotnikov. It was clear that the *politsai* on top of the hill had an excellent view of the man lying alone in the snow, and although they hadn't followed him down yet, they would obviously be able to finish him off with rifle-fire. And if Rybak went to rescue him, they would both certainly be killed. He'd seen the same thing happen during the Finnish campaign, when the bastards had killed four or five men in the space of a minute in this same simple way. When one man was shot, the next in the line dashed out to help him and was brought down alongside him, and then the next crawled out to help them. Every man who went out must have known what was going to happen, but no one could refrain from trying to help his wounded comrades.

He had to get away while there was still a chance: Sotnikov was beyond help. Rybak slung his rifle on his shoulder again, hoisted the sheep on to his back and, stumbling over the tussocky ground, set off along the edge of the swamp.

He got some way before he had to stop again, exhausted. There had been no shots for some time, and as he listened to the silence he guessed, with a strange feeling of relief, that it was all over. But after a moment or two there was a further burst of firing. There were three shots, and one bullet sang over the marsh. So Sotnikov was still alive. The unexpected shots threw Rybak into new alarm. They slowed his flight down to a more cautious pace, and made his danger-sharpened senses even keener. The sheep felt heavier and heavier. Its soft pliant weight seemed strangely alien and stupid. He carried it mechanically, thinking of something completely different.

In a few moments he came to a shallow, steep-sided dip—probably the bed of the frozen brook. He really should have crossed to the other bank, but as soon as he reached the edge, he slipped, dropped his load, and slid on his back in the snow to the bottom. He cursed and heaved himself back up through the soft snow. Then he suddenly knew that he couldn't go on. How could he put so much effort into carrying a sheep and leave his comrade behind? Of course Sotnikov was alive, and drawing attention to himself by firing. In fact he had covered Rybak's retreat and saved him from death, although he himself was in a very bad way. He had no chance of getting out alone, whereas for Rybak it would be easy to go off and leave him—they'd never catch up with him now.

But what could he tell them back in the forest?

He now saw clearly how despicable his first impulse had been. He swore quietly, and slumped down in anguish on the edge of the bank of the stream. There was another shot in the distance beyond the thicket, but no reply from the top of the hill. Perhaps the situation had changed. Then there was a long, heavy pause, during which Rybak's new resolution finally screwed itself up, and he jumped to his feet.

Trying not to think about the problem any more, he strode quickly back the way he had come.

6

Sotnikov hadn't any intention of shooting it out with the *politsai*. He just fell on the slope, his head spinning and everything swimming before his eyes. He was afraid that he might not be able to get up again.

From where he lay he could clearly see Rybak making all the speed he could towards the thicket, holding the sheep in position on his shoulders. Sotnikov didn't call after him because he knew it was already too late to save himself. For a few long seconds, panting from fatigue, he lay motionless, until he heard voices behind him and realised that he would soon be captured. Then he dragged his rifle out of the snow and fired into the darkness to stave off for a moment the fate that was approaching. Just to let them know that he wasn't going to give himself up that easily.

It seemed to work. They appeared to stop in their tracks, and he began to think that he ought to make another effort to get away. Although he knew that his chances were infinitesimally small, somehow or other he fought down his weakness, pulled himself together and hauled himself to his feet, leaning on his rifle. They appeared suddenly, unexpectedly close to him—three motionless silhouettes on the grey curve of the hill, looking warily in his direction. The one on the right must have spotted him, for he shouted something. Sotnikov fired a second time, almost without taking aim. He saw them shy away and drop to the ground or duck in anticipation of more shots. Then, his felt boots scuffing through the snow, he staggered off uncertainly down the snow-covered slope, risking another fall at every step. Rybak was far ahead by now. He'd almost reached the thicket; he might have a chance of escaping. He himself was doing his utmost to get off the hillside, but he had covered barely a hundred paces when three shots sounded behind him almost in a volley.

He totered a few more steps on the point of falling. Suddenly there was a searing pain in his right thigh and a slow warm moistness began to spread from his knee down into his boot. After a few more steps he lost almost all sensation in his foot, which grew heavy as lead and refused to obey him. The next moment he collapsed into the snow. He did not feel any severe pain, just a hot sensation in his chest and a burning sensation above his knee. The inside of his trouser-leg was completely soaked. For a short time he lay there biting his lip until it hurt. His earlier fear had vanished from his mind. He didn't even feel regret any more. His only thought now was a calm, detached awareness—so detached that it seemed to come from outside himself—of the inevitability of fast-approaching death. It was a little surprising that it should have struck so suddenly, when he was least expecting it. Death had passed him by countless times before in the most desperate situations, but this time it could not miss him.

He heard more voices behind him—probably the *politsai* moving in to take him dead or alive. The pain in his leg sharpened acutely, and he was barely able to master it enough to raise himself on his hands and sit upright. The skirts of his greatcoat, his sleeves and his knees were thickly covered in snow, and the bloodstain on his trouser-leg was spreading. But he paid no attention to that—he worked the bolt of his rifle, extracted the empty magazine and put a round in the breech.

Again he saw the three on the slope, one ahead and two following, shadowy figures working their way down rather uncertainly from the top. Clenching his teeth, he cautiously stretched his wounded leg out in the snow, lay down and aimed more carefully than before. As the echo of the shot died away he saw all three of them go down together, and immediately the silence of the night was broken again by their return of his fire. He realised that he had delayed them and forced them to reckon with him, and this gave him a certain satisfaction. Weakened by the painful effort, he leant his head on the butt of his rifle. He was too tired to follow their movements or to try to avoid their fire. He just lay quietly, trying to gather the remains of his strength to shoot again. From above him on the hill they kept him under steady fire. A couple of times they were very close—one bullet whined over his head, and another struck the ground close to his elbow, spattering his face with snow. He didn't move. Let them kill him. What does it matter if they do . . .? But as long as he was still alive he wasn't going to let them get near him.

He wasn't afraid of death in battle—he'd lived through that fear a dozen times in tight corners, nor was he especially attached to his own life, which had long since ceased to be a pleasure, or even, recently, an obligation. As long as he'd been an army officer on whom other people's lives or the outcome of a battle depended, it had been important to stay alive. But now he was alone and there was only himself to worry about. Of course even in the partisans it wasn't as simple as all that—you had to look after yourself so as not to become a burden to the others. Take their section leader Zhamchenko, for instance. He'd been wounded by a piece of shrapnel in the stomach in the Kryzhovskii forest back in the autumn, and they'd carried him all night through the swamp past the enemy emplacements when it was hard enough work for the others to keep their own skins intact. When they'd finally got through to safety Zhamchenko had died.

That was the kind of fate that Sotnikov feared most, although it seemed that it had passed him by. Of course there was little hope of escape, but at least he was conscious and he had his rifle. That was the main thing. His leg had grown strangely numb from his thigh right down to his foot, and he could no longer feel the warmth of the blood, although he had probably lost quite a lot. The bunch up the hill fired a few more shots and then lay low for a while. But then one of them got up. The others stayed lying where they were, while the third moved rapidly down the slope and disappeared. Sotnikov stretched for his rifle again and realised how badly he had been weakened. His leg was beginning to hurt more. Strangely, it was his knee and the tendon below it which hurt most, although he knew that the bullet had struck higher, in the thigh. He clenched his teeth and turned slightly on to his left side to take part of his weight off the right. At that moment another shadow flickered briefly down the slope—evidently they were following army tactical rules precisely and closing in on him in short dashes. He waited until the third shadow rose, and fired, more or less at random—his sights were hard to make out in the darkness. Once again there was a burst of fire in return, this time at least ten shots. When they died away, he took a new magazine from his pocket and reloaded the rifle. He would have to make his ammunition last. He had only fifteen rounds left.

He probably lay a long time in the snow. His body began to freeze, and the pain in his leg increased. The cold and the loss of blood brought on a fit of shivering. It was torture to have to wait. After the last lot of shots the enemy had kept quiet, as if they'd melted away into the night. There was no sign of them on the hillside. They would hardly have left him here—they must still be trying to take him dead or alive. Then he began to imagine that they were stalking him, or that his sight was beginning to go. Dark spots danced before his eyes, from exhaustion. He was afraid that he might lose consciousness and that the worst thing that he could imagine, that he had ever imagined throughout the war, might happen, the thing he had to preserve his last scrap of strength to prevent—he must not be taken alive.

He raised his head cautiously. Something flickered across the frosty darkness. He thought it was a man. Then he realised with relief that it was just a dried blade of grass blown by the wind across his sights. He moved his wounded leg and bit back a groan as it was immediately slashed by a convulsing pain. He eased his knee slightly. He no longer had any feeling at all in his toes. But to hell with his toes, they weren't going to be any use to him any more. His other leg was perfectly all right.

He might have been lying there a long time, or then again he might not—he had lost all sense of time. Only one thought concerned him now—he mustn't let himself be taken by surprise. He suspected that they were crawling up on him and he picked up his rifle again and fired another shot in their general direction to hold them back. But the *politsai* did not return his fire at once, and he wondered whether they might have dropped down into one of the gulleys that ran down the hillside and had temporarily lost sight of him. He decided to take advantage of this brief breathing space and turned painfully on to his side.

His boot had frozen and was very difficult to get off. It would have to be peeled away from the skin. He writhed in pain, tensed himself, clenched his jaw until his teeth ground together, and dragged the boot as hard as he could. The first attempt produced no result. After a breather he grabbed the boot with even greater determination. He got it off at the fifth or sixth attempt, and lay for several minutes totally exhausted and incapable of movement. Then he threw the boot into the snow and raised his head. He could see no one in front of him. Now let them come. He was ready to kill himself. All he had to do was to hold the muzzle of the rifle to his throat and pull the trigger with his toe. He rejoiced silently, gleefully—now they wouldn't take him alive. But he still had two full magazines, which he would use in his final battle. He raised his head higher. They must be somewhere, they couldn't be burrowing through the earth towards him.

They didn't seem to be anywhere around, or perhaps he couldn't see them in the darkness. Indeed the night seemed to be getting blacker and the moon had disappeared again. So that was how his life was going to end, at night, in the frozen open country, completely alone, no one at hand. They would take him to headquarters, search him, strip him, and bury his body in some knacker's yard. His family grave, which at one time had terrified him, now seemed an unattainable dream, almost a luxury. They would bury him, and no one would ever know whose body it was that lay there. But all this didn't matter. He had nothing left worth grieving for before the end, except perhaps his rifle which had served him impeccably since the autumn. It had never rusted, no part of the mechanism had ever let him down and it fired amazingly true and straight. The others had rapid-fire German automatic weapons, and a few had the SVT, but he had never parted with his standard issue model. It had been his best friend through the winter; now it would probably fall into the hands of some traitor in the Russian *politsai.*

His bare foot was beginning to freeze. He couldn't afford to let it get totally frost-bitten—how could he press the trigger then? He overcame the weakness and pain to adjust his position in the snow and then suddenly noticed a movement on the hill. But they weren't coming towards him, they were going away. Two barely discernible dark shadows were slowly moving back up the slope. Soon they reached the top of the hill. He couldn't understand what was going on. They were probably going back to the sleigh to get help. He didn't dare entertain the thought that they might be leaving him. But then he saw them setting off back to the road.

All the same, he couldn't hope to last long in this frost in the middle of nowhere. He would probably die slowly from the cold and loss of blood. As if he were angry with them because it was their fault, he raised his rifle to his shoulder and fired after them.

Then he realised that his fear of freezing to death alone had been unfounded. Not far off, further down the hill, a shot rang out in reply. They had left a guard behind, probably while they went for help. One man with a rifle would be enough to keep him pinned down. They had probably guessed that he was wounded and couldn't get far. So everything was back to normal.

But the situation was encouraging. He could fight on more or less even terms with one man. It was unfortunate, of course, that he couldn't see his opponent—the bastard was probably well camouflaged. And at night you couldn't make much of a guess where a man was purely from the sound of his shots. He probably had Sotnikov firmly in his sights—he would only need to lift his head for a rifle to crack in the distance. All he could do was to lie there and freeze to death. He was shivering constantly already and he felt he couldn't survive long.

But he held on, hoping for something he couldn't define, although it would have been so easy to finish it all off. Perhaps he wanted to live? He felt that he did, especially now that the others had partially lifted their siege. But how? He couldn't crawl. He tried to keep his wounded leg still. Even his good leg was beginning to freeze; soon he would have no working legs at all. And what salvation could there be without legs?

He left his rifle in the snow, turned on to his side and looked for his boot. It was lying there, its top buried in the snow. He stretched to pick it up, emptied the snow from it, and began to thrust his stiffening foot into it. But he couldn't manage to get it on—it was far harder than getting it off. His head swam with pain as soon as his foot touched the boot and he had to grit his teeth to get over the surge of agony and exhaustion. While he was trying, there was another shot and the hollow, frozen echo rang round the countryside. The shot came from the same place as before, just down the hill. A second and a third followed it. He didn't hear the bullets—indeed he was not listening for them. Lying there in the snow, he kept on trying to drag his boot on. Finally he succeeded, although his foot was not completely home. He turned his face into the snow, to cool his burning cheeks and forehead, and felt better. And then he heard in the night a voice that came from somewhere he couldn't place:

'Sotnikov, Sotnikov . . .'

This staggered him, and he decided that he was beginning to get hallucinations. But all the same he turned round. Behind him in the darkness something real and living was crawling towards him, repeating quietly and insistently:

'Sotnikov, Sotnikov . . .'

It was Rybak, of course. Sotnikov could hear his low, worried voice clearly, and his tension slipped away. He couldn't be quite certain that it was a good thing that Rybak had come back for him—maybe both of them would be cut off now—but he realised that for the time being at least his death had been deferred.

7

They crawled to the thicket, Rybak in the lead, Sotnikov following behind. It was a long and difficult haul. Sotnikov could not keep up with him and sometimes stopped altogether, bogged down in his tracks. Then Rybak had to turn round, get hold of him by his greatcoat collar and drag him. Rybak, too, was exhausted. Apart from helping Sotnikov, he was carrying both their rifles, which kept slipping from his back and dragging in the snow. The night was darker. The moon had totally disappeared in a dark mist—this must have helped to save them. But there were a couple more shots from the hill—probably the remaining *politsai* had caught a glimpse of them.

Somehow or other they made it to the edge of the thicket and lay among the soft snow-covered tussocks of marsh grass. The dark branches of alder hid them pretty effectively in the darkness. Rybak was wet through—the snow was melting in the sleeves and collar of his sheepskin, and his back was soaked in the sweat which streamed off him. He was tired, more tired perhaps than he had ever been in his life before, and he lay helplessly face down, occasionally looking up at the face of the hill to make sure that no one was after them. But there was no one behind. Although the one *politsai* had obviously noticed movement, he had not plucked up courage enough to follow them—it would be too easy to catch a bullet himself.

'Well, how are you?' Rybak asked, still breathing out great gulps of steaming breath, which could be seen even in the darkness.

'Bad,' replied Sotnikov in a barely audible voice.

He lay on his side, his head thrown back in its frozen, closely fitting forage cap. His wounded leg lay stretched out, his knee slightly raised, shuddering nervously. Rybak swore quietly to himself.

56

'Let's get on. Otherwise they'll cut us off, and we won't be able to break through.'

He got to his feet, but before standing up to his full height he pulled his stained old towel from round Sotnikov's neck and with fingers shaking from exhaustion tied it tightly round the wounded leg above the knee. Sotnikov grunted twice from the pain and held his breath, but managed not to groan. Rybak went down on his knees and offered Sotnikov his back.

'Right, get up.'

'Wait a moment. I might be able to manage . . .'

Rolling over weakly in the snow, Sotnikov struggled on to one knee, his wounded leg dragging uselessly, and then tried to get to his feet. He succeeded.

'Well done! Now hold on!'

Rybak grabbed him by the arm, and Sotnikov was standing at last. He managed two steps, limping heavily on his wounded leg. This encouraged Rybak—if a man's on his feet, everything can't be lost. When he had crawled back to Sotnikov and discovered that he was wounded, he'd nearly gone out of his mind; what would he do in a situation like this? But now he was beginning to calm down a little; somehow or other they might manage to make it back.

With Rybak's help Sotnikov clumsily hopped along on one leg, partially supporting himself on the other. They were moving through low underbrush here, not very dense, and the snow was soft and deep. Sotnikov clung to Rybak with one hand and with the other grasped at the stiff alder branches as he walked, trying to get on as fast as he could, limping painfully on his bad leg. There was a constant, disturbing whistle in his chest, and sometimes he began to cough heavily, agonisingly. Rybak was tense, for the coughing could easily be heard a long way off. But he kept quiet. He didn't even ask Sotnikov how he was feeling, but giving himself no rest, determinedly dragged him through the trees.

After the thicket on the other side of the stream-bed and a long stretch of frozen swamp, the ground began to rise again steeply up the hillside. As they crawled diagonally up it, Rybak felt his strength ebbing away. He was no longer in any state to support Sotnikov, who was sinking heavily to the ground, and he himself was so exhausted that without a word they both flopped into the snow almost simultaneously. Breathing loudly, as if breath were the only thing that mattered, they lay for a long time on the slope, astonishingly indifferent to everything. Rybak knew that any minute the *politsai* might appear, and was listening for their shouts, but despite this his body was quite unable to overcome the crippling exhaustion that had seized it.

Maybe a quarter of an hour later, when he had got his breathing under better control, Rybak turned on his side. Sotnikov, beside him, was trembling slightly in a fever.

'Got any ammo left?'

'One magazine,' Sotnikov muttered, wheezing.

'Then we can defend ourselves.'

'Not for long.'

True enough, you can't hold out for long with twenty rounds, thought Rybak, but he couldn't see any other way out. They couldn't allow themselves to be taken prisoner—they would have to fight to the last.

'Where the hell did they come from?' Rybak began to go back over what had happened with renewed vehemence. 'It's true what they say: troubles never come singly.'

Sotnikov lay silent beside him, forcing himself not to groan. His face darkened by the cold, drawn with pain, the stubble of his beard covered in hoar-frost from his breath, suddenly seemed to Rybak to belong to someone he did not know, and this shocked him. He began to realise that his companion was in a really bad way.

'Does it hurt a lot?'

'It does,' Sotnikov growled.

'Hang on,' said Rybak with gruff sympathy, suppressing an unasked-for and entirely inappropriate feeling of pity. He sat up in the snow and started anxiously to examine the terrain, which seemed wholly unfamiliar. There was a stretch of hummocky open land and a small birch grove a little way off, but he hadn't the faintest idea where the big forest which they needed so badly could be. After the twisting and turning in their efforts to shake off pursuit in the scrub, he had lost all track of where they were or which way they ought to be moving to get back to their camp.

This brought a new fear into his mind—they were in trouble enough without getting lost in the night. He felt like discussing this with Sotnikov, but Sotnikov was stretched out in the snow as if he could no longer feel fear, or even the cold wind which had become still more unbearable now that they were out of the shelter of the trees. For the moment exhaustion kept them pinned to the ground, and Rybak gazed anxiously into the surrounding darkness, wondering which way to turn.

He tried to decide this by going back in his mind over the tortuous track they had followed to get here, while his instinct for self-preservation urged him to get as far away as possible from the undergrowth where the *politsai* had picked them up. It occurred to him that the *politsai* might well follow their tracks to where they lay, and that accordingly they should move further along the way they were going.

When he had finally let himself be convinced by this reasoning, Rybak stood up and slung both rifles on his shoulder.

'Come on, let's see what we can do . . .'

Sotnikov began to try to drag himself to his feet. Rybak attempted once again to help him, but once he was on his feet, he shook his arm free of Rybak's supporting hand.

'Give me my rifle!'

'Do you think you can manage on your own?'

'I'll give it a try.'

You just do that, thought Rybak, handing over the rifle with a feeling of relief. Leaning on it like a crutch, Sotnikov moved a few paces, and very slowly they set off across the snow.

An hour later they had got a long way from the swamp and were dragging themselves blindly along the slope of a hillside. Rybak felt that the dawn was near, that the last moments of night were running out, and that their chances of success were receding. If morning found them in open country, they were almost certainly finished.

They had been helped so far by the fact that the snow was only lying shallow, and their feet didn't break through as often as they had in the swamp. There were dried-up clusters of marsh grass poking through the snow, in some places quite thickly. Rybak avoided these spots and tried to pick a way where the snow was less deep, keeping away from low-lying patches for fear of plunging into drifts. The higher ground was safer. But their tracks showed up far too clearly in the snow. Once when he looked back, Rybak felt quite alarmed—it would have been easy to follow them, even by night. As he gazed around him he thought that no matter how dangerous the road might be, the road that had almost been their undoing during the night, they really ought to get back on to it. It was only on the road that their tracks would mingle with other people's, and thus avoid giving the *politsai* a clear lead straight back to the partisan encampment.

Meanwhile the darkness was beginning to lift just enough for them to be able to make out the snow-covered ground, broken here and there by dark clumps of undergrowth and an occasional tree. At one point Rybak saw something which he couldn't define at first, but which, as he approached, turned out to be a boulder. There was no sign of a road at all. He turned sharply off, uphill. It was hard going, but there was always the chance that once they got to the top they would suddenly find the forest. Once they were there they would be able to hide; it was unlikely that the *politsai* would follow them in straight away. They would have to think twice before plunging into the forest, and that would give them a chance of getting away from their pursuers.

It wasn't the first time Rybak had found himself in this kind of situation and up to now he had always managed to get out of it somehow. In this kind of mess the things that counted were speed and ingenuity; the only correct decision was the one taken without a moment's delay. Now that the *politsai* had let them off the hook for some unknown reason, there was a similar opportunity and he would have been able to take full advantage of it if it hadn't been for Sotnikov. But there wasn't much chance of getting far with Sotnikov. They hadn't even made the top of the hill before Sotnikov was seized with yet another fit of coughing which bent him double, and for several minutes his body heaved and twisted as if in vain attempts to expel something out of his system. Rybak stopped, turned back to his companion, and tried to support him by the arm. But Sotnikov was finding it hard to stand, and in the end Rybak lowered him to the hard windswept surface of the snow.

'Wait a moment, let's have a breather!'

'Bad, is it?'

'It's obvious we're not going to get out of this.'

Rybak didn't reply—he didn't want to get involved in that kind of discussion, didn't want to have to ladle out insincere encouragement or consolation. He certainly couldn't think of a way out himself, nor even which way to go.

For a moment he stood over Sotnikov, who lay motionless and twisted on his side, his wounded leg beneath him. In Rybak's mind, his feelings for Sotnikov began to grow confused. There was an unwilling pity that one man had to bear so much—not merely to be ill, but to be wounded as well—but at the same time he began to feel a kind of superstitious anger, as if the man had brought a kind of curse on both of them. In this rapid mental turmoil Rybak began to think more and more of himself, and one emotion at times submerged all' the rest—fear for his own life. True, whenever the thought began, he tried to rid himself of it and to remain calm. To fear for his own life was the first step on the road to complete confusion. You only need to feel sorry for yourself, to worry, for troubles to start piling up and that'd put the lid on everything. Although things were certainly sticky at the moment, all was not necessarily lost.

'Right, you wait here.'

Rybak left Sotnikov in the snow and hauled himself up the slope to have a look round. He was still hopeful that the forest might lie over the crest of the hill. They had come a long way during the night, and if only they'd been moving in the right direction, they must be somewhere near it.

It was a pity that the moon had set altogether. He couldn't see any distance—the night was swimming in a frosty mist, and the pre-dawn shadows were writhing around him. But all the same it was clear that there was no forest anywhere near. From the crest of the hill stretched open country with a few low hills and what was probably a thicket, and a very small thicket at that, darkly outlined on a gentle slope. Everywhere he could see dim shapes, dark clumps of woods, and indistinct silhouettes of bushes. Then in the snowy darkness he made out a short curved line on the ground; he glimpsed it briefly then it disappeared as the mist closed in. He moved quickly towards it, suddenly much less tired, realising that the line in the snow was the dark surface of a road. He saw that it was well used, with deep ruts and hoof marks. He had never seen a more welcome sight in his life. He turned and ran lightly down the slope to Sotnikov, lying motionless and twisted in the snow.

'The road's up there. Can you hear me?'

Sotnikov blearily raised his round head, which looked unnaturally small in the close-fitting forage cap, and began to try to get to his feet.

'We'll turn off the road somewhere, and they'll never find us. We *must* make it—if only we don't stumble across any more of the bastards.'

Silently, with Rybak's help, Sotnikov got up from the snow, and tried to get a firm grip of his rifle butt with fumbling fingers.

61

They slowly approached the road. Rybak peered anxiously into the darkness to make sure there was no one about. His eyes tensely swept the open country about them in a practised movement, straining hard to make out the point where the road disappeared into the night. Then, suddenly, with surprise, he noticed that the sky had grown lighter. It had turned from black to a deep blue, the stars had faded, and only the brightest could still be seen on the horizon. This sign that dawn was on its way disturbed him almost more than if he had seen someone approaching. Every instinct urged him forward, anywhere to get away from this treacherously lightening stretch of bare country. But his legs were dreadfully tired, and his companion held him back as well. Whether he liked it or not he was going to have to move slowly along the road he had just discovered—there was nothing else for it.

Accordingly he thrust down his impatient longing to hurry and gritted his teeth firmly. He said nothing to Sotnikov, who was clearly at the end of his strength, barely able to set one foot in front of the other. Rybak felt his stomach sinking—they weren't going to make it. The night was ending, and withdrawing its protection. There was nothing good to be expected of the day that was coming. With a heavy heart he watched the morning slowly and relentlessly arriving. The sky grew lighter, the gloomy expanse of snow-covered country became more and more distinct as the darkness lifted, and the road stretched further and further ahead.

They set off along the road towards the thicket.

8

Sotnikov was just as aware as Rybak that the night was drawing to an end, and he understood perfectly well what this early and unwelcome dawn might mean for them.

But he kept going. He summoned up the last remaining shreds of strength his body was capable of giving, propped himself on his rifle, and with great effort and difficulty kept his feet moving. His thigh hurt abominably, and he could not feel his feet at all. One felt boot, the one that was soaked in blood, had frozen and gone as hard as a rock—the other, which was only half pulled on, had bent right under his foot, and dragged awkwardly in the snow. Sotnikov knew that once it grew light they would almost certainly be caught, but this no longer caused him any particular alarm—he was completely indifferent to everything but his pain, his real, incessant and indescribable torture.

If it hadn't been for Rybak he would probably have given up the tormenting struggle long ago. But now, after everything that Rybak had done for him, Sotnikov felt a kind of obligation to show that he appreciated his companion's efforts.

As they moved towards the wood it grew even lighter. They began to be able to see the country around, the low hills lying under the snow. On the left, a long way from the road, down in the valley, there were some sparse trees and shrubs, but it looked as if that was the cover they had just left. The big forest which they needed so desperately to find was nowhere, not even on the horizon. It was as if it had simply sunk into the ground during the night.

As usual, Rybak kept pressing ahead, which was hardly surprising. They were on a razor's edge—at any second they might be spotted, pursued and caught. Fortunately the road was still deserted. The clump of pine trees ahead drew nearer, although very slowly. As he struggled along, leaning on his rifle butt and limping heavily, Sotnikov occasionally forgot his pain long enough to look impatiently at the trees. He longed to reach them, not merely because of the shelter they would give them from the road, but because he would have a chance to rest.

They had barely got halfway towards the clump when Rybak swore and stood stock still as if nailed to the road.

'Hell! It's a cemetery.'

Sotnikov raised his head, looked and nodded. True enough, the clump of pines which they had taken to be a natural thicket was in fact a village burial ground. Under the low-hanging branches of the pines they could now make out a few wooden crosses, a low fence and a small brick monument on a low mound in the centre of the graveyard. But the worst thing was that beyond the pine trees they could see the thatched roofs of a nearby village; a spiral of smoke from the chimneys drifted into the sky.

Rybak blew his nose with his fingers and wiped it on the back of his hand.

'Well, what do we do?'

There was clearly nowhere else to go, and they couldn't just stand there in the middle of the road. So, still more weary and anxious, they dragged themselves along towards the village.

At first they were lucky, or so it seemed. The village was probably only just beginning to wake up, and they made it to the cemetery without meeting anyone on the way. There were plenty of tracks around here, both on the road and just off it to the side. They hurried as best they could along a pathway which they could just make out in the snow under the overhanging pine branches. Usually Sotnikov found gloomy places like this vaguely alarming and repulsive and tried to avoid them, but this particular graveyard seemed to have been sent by God for their salvation—where else would they have been able to hide in full view of the village?

They moved quickly past the raw earth of a child's grave, so recent that it wasn't even covered with snow, until they reached a place where the pines and some low fences hid them from the windows of the village houses. The going was easier here. Sotnikov used his hands to help him, clutching at crosses, at the low-hanging branches, or at the fence to haul himself along. When they had got some way from the road, he leant against the sturdy trunk of one of the pines and let himself sink heavily into the snow. If only he could feel well and rested once more, if only the pain could somehow be taken from his leg—that would be absolute divine bliss. After that dreadful night every fibre in him was frozen, had turned into a relentless agony, and his confused mind was now barely aware of what was going on, of the world and his situation in it. He realised, of course, that his condition was distinctly unenviable, and perhaps even hopeless, and his greatest distress came from his helplessness, his total incapacity to alter anything for the better. Mind and consciousness counted for little now. All that mattered was sheer physical strength, precisely the thing he hadn't got.

He lay there, his back propped against the rough bark of the pine trunk, and covered his eyes with his hand, so as not to look at Rybak and not to have to talk to him. He felt almost guilty that his sufferings had exposed his companion to risk. Without him, of course, Rybak would have been miles away already. Rybak was fit, he was more anxious to live than Sotnikov, who was not at all surprised by Rybak's relentlessly determined efforts to save him throughout the previous night. He accepted all Rybak's efforts as of right. He regarded them as part of the mutual assistance that soldiers can expect from one another, and had Rybak's help been offered to anyone else, he would have had nothing against it. But for himself, although he was wounded, he wanted desperately to refuse to admit that he was weak, that he needed anybody's help—for some reason his whole being revolted against the idea. At best he could have looked after himself, and where that wasn't possible he tried to restrict dependence on anybody else—and that meant any dependence on Rybak.

But Rybak, who clearly wasn't aware of what was going on in Sotnikov's mind, went on worrying about him. When they had rested a little, he said, 'Wait here, and I'll go down to the village. There's a farm cottage quite close; if anything happens we can hide up in the barn.'

I don't mind waiting, thought Sotnikov. Just as long as I don't have to move! He was quite happy to wait for a long time, provided that something good turned up in the end. Rybak rose wearily to his feet and picked up his rifle. So that it should not be too obvious what it was, he held it like a walking stick, by the barrel, and strode out over the snow-covered mounds of the graves. Sotnikov opened his eyes, turned on his side, and drew his rifle closer to him. Between the trunks of the pine trees quite close to them he could see the last hut in the village, and a dilapidated shed near by. A tattered old rag caught on the rickety fence flutered in the wind. It looked as if no one lived there.

Rybak soon disappeared from his field of view, but everything was still quiet and peaceful in the village. Sotnikov tried to arrange his injured leg more comfortably and in doing so caught hold of one of the posts of the grave surround. The post came away in his hand. The grave was old, probably long since abandoned. There was just a single stone, not even a cross. The rotting fence round the grave had lived out its time—the last surviving memorial of a man on earth. Suddenly this village burial ground made Sotnikov feel unbearably depressed, among these graves, and memorial stones, and rotting, rickety crosses. As he looked at them he wondered, with gloomy irony, why? This old-fashioned custom of raising memorials was nothing more than man's naive attempt to continue his existence on earth after death. But was that really possible? And why should it be necessary?

No, life was the only thing that really mattered. In the future, when human society was more perfect, everything would be measured against the value of human life. And every individual life would be of supreme importance to society as a whole, because the strength and harmony of society would depend on the happiness of each single member of society. And as for death—well, you can't avoid death. The main thing is to get rid of violent, premature death, and give man a chance of using to the full, sensibly and purposefully, the limited span he is given in this world. For man, despite his incredible strength, will probably long continue to be so physically weak that a tiny fragment of metal will be enough to deprive him of his unique and precious life.

But the spiritual reserves of the human mind were something of a consolation. Sotnikov would never forget that summer in the German P.o.W camp, when the S.S had been interrogating an elderly grey-haired Russian colonel, seriously wounded in the fighting, his arms broken, barely a breath of life left in him. The colonel didn't seem to understand the meaning of the word fear. He refused to answer their questions, and showered insults on Hitler, fascism and Germany. The Gestapo officer could have killed him with his bare hands, or shot him, as an hour before he had shot two political officers from the infantry, but he didn't even reply to the colonel's insults. It was as if this was the first time he had come across anything like it, and it had taken him completely aback.

Then he grabbed the telephone, reported to his superiors and waited for a decision from higher authority. Of course, they did shoot the colonel then, but those few minutes before the execution were his triumph, his last action, probably a more difficult one than any he had fought in battle. The colonel hadn't known that anyone from his own side could hear his defiance. It just happened that Sotnikov was in the next hut, listening through a thin wall.

As the frost bit slowly but remorselessly into his bones, Sotnikov patiently turned to look down the side of the cemetery, where he immediately spotted Rybak as he came into view. Instead of coming straight across the field, he was cautiously working his way along the fence, probably so as to stay out of sight of the village. Then he turned towards Sotnikov. A moment later he reached him, and fell panting under the pine.

'It looks OK. There's a cottage with the door unlocked. I listened, and there's no sound of anyone inside . . .'

'Well?'

'Well, you know . . . maybe if I took you down, we could get warm, and then . . .'

Rybak didn't finish his sentence, but just looked out at the morning-lit stretch of open country. They could see a long way already. His voice sounded uncertain, almost guilty. Sotnikov guessed what was worrying him.

'It's all right. I'll stay there and you go back.'

'It'll be better that way.' Rybak sounded a lot more cheerful. 'I'll be off. The only thing is, I can't make out where the damned forest is. We've got ourselves lost.'

'You'll have to ask.'

'We'll ask. And you can hold on here for a while. Then perhaps we can get somewhere better. Safer.'

'OK, OK,' answered Sotnikov in a deliberately cheerful voice.

'And don't you worry, I'll sort it out. Get someone to look after you, and all that.'

Sotnikov didn't reply. Everything that Rybak was proposing was logical and right, and yet Sotnikov felt somehow hurt. He realised of course that this was because he was weak, a result of that terrible night. What was there to feel hurt about? They were equal and independent, and neither had any obligation towards the other. And even so, thank God, Rybak had done everything possible for him. You might even say that he'd saved his life in the most

impossible circumstances, and now it was time for Sotnikov to let
him go.

'Right, let's go then, while there's no one around.'

Sotnikov tried to get to his feet, but when he moved his
wounded leg he was enveloped in a sheet of pain so intense that he
stretched out in the snow. After a moment he pulled himself
together and, gritting his teeth, heaved himself up.

They left the cemetery and moved down below the hill through
the young pines. Soon they came to a well-trodden path which took
them down to an unfenced farmyard. A little way off from the
cluster of houses which formed the village was quite a big old
deserted cottage, its corners plastered with clay and its broken
window stuffed with a piece of old rag. Sure enough, the blackened
hasp on the door was loosely secured by a scrap of wood—it looked
as if someone had just left to go not far away and there was no one
in the house. Sotnikov thought that that might well be to the good.
At least it got over the difficulty of having to explain straight away
who they were, which was never pleasant or easy in this kind of
situation.

Rybak removed the chip of wood from the latch and let himself
and Sotnikov into the passageway. It was dark. There were piles of
tubs and household junk by the walls, and a huge rusty tin trunk. In
the corner was a pair of millstones. Sotnikov had once before come
across this clumsy rustic tool for grinding corn, two round stones in
a shallow box with a rod to turn them fastened to the upper one. A
small window in the wall, covered in a spider's web, let in enough
light for them to find the inner door.

Sotnikov managed to get to the door by working his way along
the wall, and with Rybak's help negotiated the high threshold. As
they entered the room they were greeted by a mixture of household
smells, and warmth. He stretched out his hand to the peeling, rusty
side of the stove. It had just been lit, and his body was filled with
such a feeling of bliss that he let out a groan, the first, probably, that
he had allowed himself throughout this terrible night. Utterly
exhausted, he lowered himself clumsily on the short bench by the
stove, almost stumbling over some full pots standing on the floor.
While he was arranging his leg, Rybak looked behind the striped
matting which was hung over the door into the other half of the
cottage. There was a slight sound of a bed squeaking. Then another.
Sotnikov pricked his ears. Now the most crucial question was about

to be resolved.

'Are you alone here?' Rybak asked in a firm voice, standing in the doorway.

'Yes.'

'Where's your father?'

'He's gone away.'

'And your mother?'

'Mummy's gone to do some threshing at Uncle Emelian's. To earn money. There are four of us to feed, and she's on her own.'

'Well, you seem to know all about it. And the other mouths she has to feed are all asleep, are they? OK, let them sleep.' Rybak was speaking more quietly. 'What can you find to feed us on?'

'Mummy cooked some potatoes this morning,' replied the child's voice, anxious to volunteer information.

There was the sound of bare feet on the floor, and a girl of ten or so with tousled hair, wearing a longish, much mended dress, looked out from behind the curtain. She gazed briefly at Sotnikov from her dark eyes, but she didn't seem to be frightened. She went over to the stove and stretched up to the high shelf. So as not to be in her way, Sotnikov cautiously moved his leg to one side.

By the window there was an unlaid table and a bench with an earthenware dish on it. The girl put the dish on the table and shook some boiled potatoes into it from the pot she had brought from the stove. The movements of her small hands were jerky, even clumsy, but it was clear that she was doing her best to welcome the guests. She produced a knife from a washing up bowl concealed in a dark corner, and put a plateful of big wrinkled pickled cucumbers on the table. Then she went back to the stove and watched these armed, bearded, no doubt frightening men, whom nevertheless she clearly found of absorbing interest, with silent curiosity.

'Well, let's get something inside us,' Rybak said, moving over to the table.

Sotnikov had still not got warm, and his frozen body was shaking with fever, but a delicate, aromatic steam was rising from the potatoes on the table, and he rose from the bench. Rybak helped him over to the table, and arranged his leg on the bench. It was more comfortable that way. Sotnikov took a warm potato, slightly burnt on one side, and leant his back against the whitewashed plank wall. The girl stood as deferentially as ever in the doorway to the next room, and fingering the hem of the curtain kept on gazing at them from her dark eyes, which flickered from one to another.

'Is there no bread, then?' asked Rybak.

'Lenik ate it all yesterday. While we were waiting for Mummy to come home.'

Rybak fished around inside his sheepskin, produced the hunk of bread he had lifted the previous evening from the village headman and broke a piece from it. Then he broke off another and handed it silently to the girl. She accepted it, but didn't eat it. She took it behind the partition and came back to the stove.

'Has your mother been threshing for long?' Rybak asked.

'She started the day before yesterday. She'll be working for a week yet.'

'I see. Are you the oldest?'

'Oh, yes. I'm the biggest. Katya and Lenik are only little, and I'm nine.'

'That's very old. Aren't there any Germans here?'

'They came once. We were out for a walk with Mummy and Auntie Helena. They took our piglet, the spotted one. Took him away in their car.'

Sotnikov managed to swallow a couple of potatoes and started coughing again, the same old cough. It kept on for five minutes, until it seemed that his chest was bound to burst. Then it eased a little, but he couldn't face another potato. He just drank half a mug of water and closed his eyes. His thoughts began to swim and dissolve, a painfully sweet fatigue overtook him and he drifted towards sleep. The voices of Rybak and the girl sounded very far away in his confused mind.

'What's your mother's name?'

'Demchikha.'

'So your father's Demyan?'

'That's right. Mummy's other name's Avginya.'

He heard the bench squeak under Rybak's weight—probably leaning over to take another potato—and his boots scrape the floor under the table. The conversation paused for a moment, and then the child's voice came—ingratiating, with a sly curiosity:

'Uncle, are you partisans?'

'What's that got to do with you? Nosey creature!'

'I know you're partisans.'

'Well, if you know, hold your tongue.'

'The other uncle's been wounded, hasn't he?'

'Wounded or not, not a word about it. Right?'

The girl didn't reply, and for a moment the conversation flagged.

'Shall I go and get Mummy?'

As Sotnikov drifted off to sleep, the voices of Rybak and the girl were replaced by other voices, voices from the past.

'Sit down and shut up, or else you'll get yourself stuck in the shit.'

'Shit on them all. Are we people or cattle?'

'We used to be people.'

Sotnikov's mind just managed to register the shift from the present to memory. He could see the lieutenant, wounded in the leg, limping in the long line of prisoners, leaning on the shoulder of a stronger comrade. The lieutenant's head was bandaged. The bandage was old and dirty, and there was a congealed clot of blood on his forehead. His dried lips and the unhealthy, feverish gleam in his reddened eyes gave his drawn face an appearance of semi-madness. His wounded leg gave off such a stench that Sotnikov retched slightly—the sweet odour of decay poisoned the air five yards around him. They were being marched into the wood—a meagre pine-grove just off the road. Beneath their feet they could feel the fine white sand, sprinkled with pine-needles, and the midday sun beat down pitilessly on them.

The rumour was they were going to be shot.

It looked as if it might be true. The column included the pick of the thousands in the camp—the political officers, the Party members, the Jews, and others for one reason or another suspected by the Nazis. Sotnikov was among them because he had tried to escape. There on the sand-hills in the pine-grove they would be shot. They felt sure of this because as they turned off the road, their guards clustered more closely round them and began to shout louder, trying to work the column into a tighter grouping. Up on the hill they could see soldiers standing, waiting to do their job in an efficient and economical way. But even Germans have shambles. The column was still moving towards the hillock when the guards started a shouting match with the ones who were on the edge of the pine-grove, and the prisoners were ordered to sit down, which usually happened when the Nazis wanted to stop moving. So they dropped down for a sunbathe, and waited under the snouts of the machine-guns for something to happen.

For the last few days Sotnikov had been close to the end of his tether. He felt dreadful, weak from lack of food and water, and he had totally lost faith in people. After everything that had happened, he had no further interest in going on living. His insides were dehydrated from lack of water; there was no water, just as there was no hope of salvation. He thought let's get it over with as quickly as possible, so we suffer less. For when death comes as a release from suffering, it is no longer something to be feared—it will be a sad necessity, nothing more. In silence, half in a dream, he sat among the dense crowd of men on the prickly, dry grass without any particular thoughts in his head, and that was probably why he did not immediately grasp the sense of the feverish muttering going on beside him. 'Just one. Let me get my hands on just one of them.' 'Wait a bit. Wait and see what happens.' 'It's obvious what's going to happen.' Sotnikov cautiously glanced towards the voices. His neighbour, the lieutenant he'd noticed earlier, was pulling an ordinary penknife, unseen by the others, from the filthy bandages round his leg. His eyes looked so determined that Sotnikov thought to himself, There'll be no holding that man. He's certain to leap out and do something stupid—after all, what else can he do with a knife like that? The man he was talking to, an elderly man from the staff, with no badges of rank on his battledress tunic, looked in alarm at the guards. The two nearest had come together to share a lighter, while one on horseback a little further off was keeping a watchful eye on the column.

They sat in the sun for maybe a quarter of an hour more, until there was an order from the hill and the guards began to try to get the column back on its feet. Sotnikov knew what his neighbour had decided to do. The lieutenant began to work his way towards the outside of the column, close to one of the guards. The man he had selected was a strong, stocky German, carrying, as they all did, a machine-gun slung across his chest, wearing a dark tunic with sweat-stained armpits. His forage cap was damp at the edge as well, and the hair that stuck out from under it was scarcely Aryan—it was a dark, greasy forelock. The German hastily finished his cigarette, spat into the sand, and moved two paces closer to the column apparently with the intention of driving the prisoners back into line. At that moment the lieutenant, like a vulture swooping, leapt on him from behind and plunged his knife up to the hilt into his sunburnt neck.

The German let out a short, harsh grunt, and dropped like a

72

stone. Someone yelled, 'Get the hell out of it!' and a few men hurled themselves into the field as if propelled by springs. Sotnikov froze for a second, the whole thing had happened so unexpectedly, but then gave way to a wild impulse of self-preservation, and also flung himself off the road. Indeed he almost stumbled over the lieutenant, who had started to run but tripped and fell on his side right under Sotnikov's feet, slashing his knife deep across his stomach. Stonikov leapt over his body, almost catching his foot on his convulsively clenched hand, from which the tiny knife with a blade the size of a man's forefinger fell into the sand, the wet blood on the blade flashing briefly in the sun.

The Germans were thrown into confusion for about five seconds, no more, and then they began to fire. The first bursts passed over his head, but he kept on running. Surely he had never before run so fast, at such a lunatic speed. A few long strides took him to the hillock covered in pine-trees. There was now a dense hail of bullets sweeping through the pines, showering him with needles, but he kept on running without knowing where he was going, just getting as far from them as he could, while all the time a voice inside him kept on repeating in astonished delight, 'I'm alive, I'm alive.'

Unfortunately, the pine wood turned out to be a narrow strip, and not very long. After he had run a hundred paces he was out of it and into a stubble field with stacks arranged in neat rows. There was nowhere for him to hide, so he set off across the field towards a green grove of alders.

He was soon spotted, shouts broke out behind him, and someone fired. The bullet glanced off an empty cigarette-case in his trouser pocket, cutting it in two and leaving Sotnikov feeling as if he had been hit by a whiplash. He looked over his shoulder as he ran, and saw behind him a mounted German bent low over the mane of his horse, brandishing a pistol in his right hand. Well, a man can't run faster than a horse. Sotnikov thought to himself right, and turned to face his pursuer. The horse almost bowled him over, but at the last moment he twisted away from its hooves and hurled himself behind the nearest stack in the row. The German leant over in the saddle and flung out his arm. The shot cut the string which held one of the sheaves together, and the tightly packed straw sprayed out on the stubble. But Sotnikov wasn't hurt. He desperately grabbed a stone from the ground at his feet—an ordinary stone, about the size of a man's fist, dodged the charging horse again and hurled the stone straight at the face of the rider, who fired this time before he had had time to aim, and the shot went wide. Seeing salvation in these stones, Sotnikov began to snatch them up from the ground and hurl them at the German, who twisted and pirouetted on his wild-eyed horse, trying to get in a decent shot. He fired twice more, but neither shot hit the fugitive, who, pleased by his success, dashed off towards the next row of stacks.

While the German was trying to get his rearing horse under control, Sotnikov made the ten yards to the next row and turned to get another blow. This time he hit the horse's head, and the German missed again. Sotnikov hurled three more stones at him, ducking away from the flying hooves and dodging from stack to stack. But then he reached the end of the row and crouched exhausted behind the last stack, a stone clutched in his hand. This time the German rode his horse straight at the stack, as if he were determined to crush the fugitive under his hooves. The horse reared high and with foam pouring from its jaws jumped awkwardly, knocking down the stack and showering Sotnikov with sheaves. As he fell he noticed with delight that the pistol in the German's hand had been jolted by the jump, the breech had flown open and the magazine had fallen out. Realising what had happened, he reined in furiously, and Sotnikov dashed as fast as he could towards the thicket which by now was quite close. He got to the alders. Once in their shelter he had no need to worry about the horse. He paid no attention to the shots which had started again behind him, or to the branches which lashed his face, but kept on running until he reached the swamp. There was nowhere else to go. He lurched into a quagmire and sank up to his neck. He couldn't haul himself out. But at least if he didn't drown, he could consider himself saved. He froze, up to his chin in water, hanging on to a birch twig as thin as a finger, wondering whether it would hold or not. If the twig broke, he was done for. But the twig gave him enough support to keep his head above water, and gradually he recovered his strength. As soon as the shooting died down behind him he was able to heave himself out on to dry ground.

It was night now. He located the Pole Star, and hardly able to believe that he was saved, set off to the east.

9

Sotnikov lay quite still on the bench. He looked asleep. Rybak sat nearer the window and settled down to watch the path outside from behind the window-frame. The potatoes had taken the edge off his hunger, and he had nothing to do. But he couldn't leave the cottage—he had to wait. And everyone knows that the worst thing in the world is having to wait and then trying to make up for lost time. It was probably because of this that he was beginning to feel angry, although there wasn't anyone for him to feel angry with. He couldn't very well direct his anger at Sotnikov. He certainly couldn't leave him here with just the children to look after him. Their mother still wasn't back, and he could hardly send for her—how can you trust a child in a situation like this?

So he sat by the window, not knowing what he was waiting for and listening to the occasional sounds from inside the cottage. On the other side of the partition the children were getting up. He could hear their muttered squabbling in bed, and occasionally the matting over the door moved a trifle and a grubby, inquisitive face would appear briefly in the crack and then disappear hurriedly. The older girl bossed them around and wouldn't let them out from behind the partition.

Rybak examined the path outside the house in minute detail. He noted the positions of the broken-down fence and the edge of the cemetery with its border of spiky bushes. The rag which blocked the broken pane in the window kept him pretty well hidden from outside. On the damp, rotting window-sill there were a few filthy empty medicine bottles, a hank of linen thread, and a rag doll, whose eyes and mouth were drawn unskilfully in ink. At the table Sotnikov breathed uneasily in his sleep. He should be made more comfortable, but Rybak needed the housewife to help him with that. Fed up and nervous with waiting, Rybak listened almost

75

disdainfully to his companion's unhealthy breathing. Their appalling luck of the previous night was making him feel more and more depressed. It was all Sotnikov's fault. Rybak was not a man to bear a grudge, but because he was never ill himself he didn't pay much attention to other people's sickness; he couldn't even understand how people managed to catch colds, fall ill and take to their beds. And to fall ill in wartime, he thought, was about as stupid as you could get.

During his long service in the army he had come almost to despise the weak and the sick and people who for whatever reason were failures, who couldn't do this, that or the other. For his part, he tried to be able to do everything. Until the war came, sure enough, there had been things he had found difficult, particularly things to do with reading and writing—he couldn't get on with book-learning, which demanded patience and concentration. He was more a man of action, adapted to real life with all its hurry, its difficulties and its imperfections. That was probably why he'd been a sergeant for three years—he'd got plenty of character, and he wasn't short on energy either. In some ways the war made life easier for him, or at least simpler. The purpose of the struggle was clear, and he didn't worry too much about minor considerations. He knew that the more fascists you killed the better. Up to now he'd been lucky on the whole—major troubles had passed him by. In partisan life the main thing was not to lose your head, not to miss opportunities, to take decisions quickly. If you assumed that the main aim of the war was to stay alive yourself while doing as much damage to the enemy as possible, then Rybak had every right to consider himself a first-class partisan, at least as good as any of the others.

'Mummy's coming, Mummy's coming.' The children behind the parition suddenly began a happy chanting.

On the path he saw a woman coming towards the cottage with hasty, short steps. Her long dark skirt, her tattered sheepskin jacket and her shawl bundled round her head suggested that she was not in her first youth, although she didn't look all that old. Rybak kept his eye on her and cautiously moved into a better position at the window. The children's shouting disturbed Sotnikov. His bloodshot eyes flickered round the room, but when he saw that Rybak was still there, he stretched himself out on the bench again.

When he heard the latch on the outside door, Rybak moved over to the end of the bench and tried to look calm and casual. He must try to greet her as pleasantly as he could so as not to frighten or upset her. He had to get her into the right mood to persuade her to look after Sotnikov.

Before she opened the door the children poured out from behind the partition. The two girls stayed in the entrance, holding back the curtain, while a little boy of about five, barefoot, wearing ragged pants held up by little braces, dashed over to the door to meet her.

'Mummy, Mummy, the partisans have come!'

As she came in she hurried forward to pick the child up, but she suddenly straightened up and looked at the unknown men in alarmed surprise.

'Good morning,' said Rybak as amicably as he could manage.

The woman wiped the surprise from her tired face, glanced at the table and the empty dish, and her mouth hardened.

'Good morning,' she replied coldly, pushing the child away from her. 'I see you've made yourselves at home.'

'As you see. We've been waiting for you.'

'What do you want of me?'

No, there was something wrong here; the woman clearly didn't want to settle for the tone of conversation Rybak had offered her. There was a stern, unfriendly and cantankerous tone to her voice.

He didn't reply for a moment, and in the silence she unbuttoned her shabby old jacket and unwound the shawl from her head. Rybak looked at her steadily. Her straggly, ill-kempt hair, her grimy ears, her weary, greyish face—a face that was still not old, despite its network of early wrinkles around the mouth—were eloquent witnesses of the unrelieved misery of her hard life.

'Well, what do you want?' She threw her shawl on a peg near the stove and looked again at the empty bowl on the table. 'Bread are you after? Or lard? Or perhaps you'd like me to make you a nice omelette?'

'We aren't Germans,' Rybak said calmly.

'Well, who are you? Red Army men, is it? The Red Army's fighting at the front, and you're skulking around in holes and corners. Why should I be giving you potatoes and cucumbers? Galya, get hold of Lenik!' She shouted to the eldest child, and without taking her coat off she began to tidy around the stove. She put the pots back on the hot shelf at the top, took the bucket out to the passageway, and leant the broom in the corner.

At the table Sotnikov began to cough. She bent over him for a moment and frowned, but didn't speak, just went on tidying up and drew a grimy curtain across the space behind the stove. Rybak got up. He had obviously made a mistake; he should have been sterner with this quarrelsome, angry female.

'It's no use carrying on like that. We treat you decently, and all you can do is curse at us.'

'Do you call that cursing? If I were really cursing, you'd be out of here so fast your feet wouldn't touch the ground! Hey, you kids, shut up, I've trouble enough without all that racket,' she yelled at the children. 'Galya, I told you to get Lenik out of here! Lenik, I'll give you such a smack!'

'But Mummy, I only want to see the partisans!'

'I'll give you looking at partisans.' She shoved him behind the partition, and the other children vanished as well. 'Partisans, indeed.'

Rybak was watching her carefully and wondering why this Demchikha was so sharp-tongued. A mixed train of thoughts ran through his head—maybe she was married to a member of the *politsai*, or was she related to the local headman, or did she have something against the Soviets? But after a moment's though he rejected these ideas: they clearly didn't tally with the poverty-ridden life she was leading.

'Where's your Demka?' Rybak suddenly asked.

She stopped in her tracks and cautiously, almost fearfully, glanced at him.

'What do you know about Demka?'

'Oh, we know.'

'Then why ask? These days women don't know where their husbands are, do they? They just leave, and you live as best you can.'

She picked up the broom and began to sweep round the hearth. Her every movement spoke of her distaste for her unbidden guests. Rybak was pondering how best to get on to the important subject which he was waiting to raise with her.

'Now look, this man here . . .'

She straightened up and looked suspiciously at Sotnikov lying in his corner. He moved, tried to stand, and failed to suppress a groan. Demchickha stood for a moment motionless with the broom in her hands. Rybak rose from the bench where he was sitting.

78

'He's in a bad way, you see,' he said.

Sotnikov squirmed for a moment with the pain in his leg, holding his knee with both hands and gritting his teeth to stop himself moaning.

'The damn thing must have dried up.'

'Don't move. Just lie down. No one's going to send you away.'

While Rybak was arranging Sotnikov's leg on the bench, Demchikha kept on frowning, but gradually the severe expression of her face began to soften.

'He could do with something under his head,' she said. She went behind the partition and came back with a crumpled old padded jacket, with wisps of cotton-wool sticking out of the quilting. 'There, that'll be softer to lie on.'

So, Rybak thought to himself. That's a different story now. Maybe this sour old bag has some kindness in her after all. Sotnikov raised himself and she arranged the jacket under his head. He coughed and lay back again. His breathing was still quick and laboured.

'He's ill,' said Demchikha. Her voice changed completely, and she was much calmer. 'He's in a fever. Feel, he's burning.'

'That'll pass,' said Rybak, with a wave of his hand. 'That's nothing serious.'

'Oh, you wouldn't think it was serious.' The woman was getting angry again. 'Even if they shoot you, you don't think it's serious. You aren't even bothered by the thought that someone's probably killing your mother somewhere. But I've got to get some herbs boiled up for him, to get him to sweat a bit. The graveyard's not all that far off, don't forget.'

'The graveyard's not the worst thing,' Sotnikov said through his coughing.

He had livened up feverishly after his short period of half-sleep; his cheeks were flushed, probably because of his temperature. There was a febrile glitter in his eyes, and his movements had become unnaturally jerky.

'What could be worse than the graveyard?' asked Demchikha, as she cleared away the empty bowl. 'Probably you don't believe in Hell.'

'We believe in Paradise,' Rybak interjected, joking.

'If you live to see Paradise, then fine.'

The woman slammed the oven door open and began to rattle the fire-irons inside the stove. But she seemed calmer, almost as if she was beginning to approve of them. Rybak somehow felt it, everything might still turn out all right.

'It might be a good idea to wash the wound with some warm water. He's been wounded, you know.'

'I can see that for myself. That's not a dog-bite. There was shooting all night over towards Staroselye,' she said casually, leaning on the oven scraper. 'They say one of the *politsai* was killed!'

'A *politsai*?'

'Well?'

'Who says so?'

'The women were talking about it.'

'Well, if the women were talking about it, it must be true,' Rybak grinned from the end of the bench. 'They know everything.'

Demchikha looked angrily at him.

'That's right, they do. And you don't. If you did know, you wouldn't ask.' She gave him a panful of water and went through the curtained doorway to the children. 'You can do it yourself. I've got plenty to do without getting his boots off.'

'OK, OK.' Rybak agreed, and went over to Sotnikov. 'Let's get that boot off.'

Sotnikov clenched his teeth and gripped the bench with his hands, while Rybak dragged off the damp, blood-soaked boot. His trousers would have to come off as well. Sotnikov, his face screwed up with the pain, grunted:

'I'll do it myself.'

Despite the fearful pain he managed to undo his buttons and drop his blood-soaked trousers to his knees. Rybak eventually found the wound among the dried clots of blood which covered his leg. It was quite small, slightly swollen, with a blueish tinge round it. It wasn't really alarming to look at, just an ordinary bullet wound which was still bleeding slightly. There was no exit wound on the other side of the thigh, which meant that the bullet was still lodged in the leg. That made things worse.

'Yes, it's a blind wound,' said Rybak concernedly. 'We'll have to get it out.'

'OK, but you're not going to dig it out.' Sotnikov sounded irritated. 'So bandage it up. There's nothing to look at.'

'Don't worry, we'll think of something! Have you got anything

80

we could use for a bandage?' Rybak asked in a louder voice, while he began to wipe the dried blood from the leg with a damp towel.

Sotnikov's leg was trembling with the pain, but he managed to keep a grip on himself and bear it. Rybak thought that on the whole the wound didn't look too bad, unless the bullet had got the bone. If they could get the bullet out, the leg would be all right in a month. The most important thing was to find somewhere to lie up for that month so as not to fall into German hands.

Soon Demchikha appeared in the doorway holding a strip of clean cloth and Sotnikov shyly covered himself with his hands.

'Oh, don't worry. Here, take this. It's the best I can do by way of a bandage.'

While Rybak was bandaging the leg, Sotnikov gritted his teeth to keep himself from groaning, and as soon as it was finished fell back in a heap on the bench. Rybak rinsed his hands in the pan.

'Well, the operation's over. Demchikha!'

'I can see, I'm not blind,' said Demchikha, appearing in the doorway.

'Well, what next? That's the problem.' Rybak pushed his hat to the back of his head and looked at her with an anxious, questioning expression.

'How should I know what you're going to do next?'

'Well, it's obvious he can't move. That's a fact.'

'He got here all right.'

But all the same she was probably aware of what he was hinting at. They eyed each other steadily and cautiously. These prolonged looks said more than words could have done. Once again Rybak felt himself uncertain of what he was doing. The burden that he was trying to shift on to the shoulders of this woman was too heavy. It was clear that she was just as aware as he of the risk that she would be exposing herself to if she did what he wanted, and she was resisting the idea.

The conversation, which had so far been fairly lively, although leading to no kind of conclusion, flagged for a moment. Sotnikov lay on his bench silent, looking expectantly from one to the other, and Rybak cast a worried look out of the window.

'Germans!'

He leapt to the door as if he had been stung. For a fraction of a second he had glimpsed some armed men standing in the graveyard. He was sure they were standing still and not on the move, although he couldn't be sure which way they were looking. He could just see their silhouettes and the barrels of their rifles sticking up behind their backs.

Sotnikov got up from his corner and groped around him, trying to get hold of his rifle. The woman stood as if thunderstruck; the colour fled from her face and left it completely grey. At first Rybak dashed for the door, but then turned back to look out of the window.

'They're coming! Three of them are coming this way!'

It was true. Three of the men had left the graveyard and were walking, in no hurry, down to the path, no doubt following the tracks they had left earlier. As soon as Rybak saw them, his stomach tightened in painful anticipation of worse to come. He had never been so frightened before, not even last night. The best thing would be to run for it, but he looked at Sotnikov hunched on the bench, his rifle gripped in his hands, and put the thought from him. He couldn't make a break for it. Demchikha, too, apparently understood that there was no way out; suddenly she urged him in a panicky whisper:

'The loft, the loft! Climb up into the loft!'

The loft, of course, the only place to hide in a peasant's cottage. They dived into the dark passageway, where the opening to the loft could be seen dimly in the corner of the ceiling, but there was no ladder. Rybak climbed up on the round millstones. From there he threw his rifle into the loft and looked down.

'Give me yours!'

Sotnikov, his arms stretched wide, struggled through the door, supported by Demchikha. He handed over his rifle, and Rybak thrust it into the dark opening. Then he hauled Sotnikov up on to the shaky millstones, almost upsetting them. It was still a long stretch to the beam above them, but Rybak got to it somehow or other and dragged himself into the loft, his boots scraping on the wall. He turned back and grabbed Sotnikov's outstretched hands. Demchikha was helping from below, doing everything she could, although not very willingly. For half a minute or so Sotnikov wriggled weakly, grasping for his last shreds of strength, then finally he too disappeared into the loft.

'There's some flax up there. Hide behind the flax!' the woman suggested from below.

Rybak ran, crouching, over the grain which lay on the floor of

82

the loft, which, like the passageway below, was in semi-darkness, although a little light came in from the edges of the roof and from the small window in the gable end, enough for him to be able to make out the brick column of the chimney, some old clothes slung on a long pole, and a broken spinning-wheel. Further on, below the eaves, he spotted the great heap of dried flax.

'Come over here!'

Sotnikov, dragging his rifle behind him, crawled on all fours under the angle of the roof into the corner Rybak pointed out. Rybak kicked the flax roughly over him. Then Rybak himself crawled under the heap beside his companion.

For a moment they lay absolutely still, trying to get their breath back. The strong, sharp smell of flax tickled their nostrils, and the dust sprinkled their faces and worked its way into their clothes. Rybak strained his ears to see if he could make out whether the Germans were really on their tracks or whether they were merely going into the village. If they were after them, then of course there would be a search. And if there was a search they'd hardly escape it here. Sotnikov's chest was wheezing loudly, which made it harder for Rybak to hear what was going on outside, but he tried to catch the slightest sound. Now the voices were so near that Rybak froze in consternation. The Germans were talking to Demchikha.

'Hello, Frau. How's life?'

As it turned out, they were *politsai*. Rybak recognised them from the first words. Without stopping they strode across the yard, as if coming towards the door. For some reason Demchikha didn't reply, and Rybak strained to hear again, hoping desperately that they were going to pass by.

'What are you being so quiet about? Why don't you invite us in?'

'You ought to try asking them in the graveyard to invite you in, guests like you!'

There's no need to go on like that, thought Rybak regretfully. Why make them mad? Listening desperately, he was afraid that she would bring the house down round their ears by some incautious word.

'Dear, dear. Aren't you happy?'

'Happy? Goddamned radiant, that's what I am.'

'That's good. Got any vodka?'

'What d'you think this is, a shop?'

'Well, then, a couple of sausages!'

83

'Anything else you fancy? Would you like me to kill the cat to make sausages? They steal the pig and then expect me to make them sausages.'

'What a way to greet us,' another voice chimed in slyly. 'I bet you'd give any partisans that dropped by a bowl of *smetana.*'

'My own children haven't seen a drop of *smetana* for six months.'

'Well, we'll check up for ourselves.'

It was stupid to be so sharp and cocky with them. Now they hadn't gone past the house—he could hear their heavy footsteps in the passageway beneath. But it sounded as though they still hadn't opened the inner door into the cottage. Rybak was suddenly struck by the unexpected but likely prospect that they might climb straight up into the loft in search of sausages. For the meantime they were poking around the passageway, probably opening the lid of the trunk. Something fell with a clang and rolled along the ground. Scared lest a rustle might betray them, Rybak lay absolutely still, his eyes fixed on a dry, blackened rafter beam, and he thought, no, it wasn't them they were after. They were looking for food—that's what the *politsai* were usually after when they came to a village—and what they were doing in the cemetery was in all probability setting up an ambush point—they were going to patrol the road.

They were still searching the passageway when he felt Sotnikov grow unnaturally tense beside him, and the wheezing in his chest deepened. Rybak realised with cold horror that he was going to start coughing. But he didn't, he held it back somehow, and the wheezing ceased. Down below they thrust open the door, and the muffled voices came from inside the cottage.

'Where's your husband? In Moscow, is he?'

'How should I know where he is?'

'You don't know? Then we do. Stas, where's her husband?'

'Gone to Moscow, probably.'

'The bitch. Hiding things from us! She'll get thumped for that.'

'Oh, you swine!' Demchikha yelled wildly. 'May you die by the evening! May a raven peck out your eyes! May you never see your own children!'

'So that's the way it is. Stas!'

In the room below the children began to cry in fright, and the eldest girl shouted and was then silent again. Suddenly Sotnikov's tensed chest could hold back no longer. A cough burst from it like a cannon shot. Rybak felt something give way inside him, and his hands reached out for Sotnikov under the flax. Sotnikov coughed again. Down below there was a silence as complete as if everyone had left the cottage. Rybak covered Sotnikov's mouth with ferocious force, and Sotnikov subsided into noiseless writhings. But it was too late.

'Who's up there?' came the question, finally.

'No one. That cat's caught a cold, and it coughs.' He could hear Demchikha explaining fearfully. But her voice wasn't confident enough to satisfy the militia.

'Stas!' a loud hoarse voice barked.

Rybak held his breath. He realised with unusual clarity that this time everything was lost. Probably he should have defended himself, have started shooting, so that at least some of the traitors would have been killed. Yet a miracle might still happen and they could still get away.

The cottage shuddered as the door burst open and the *politsai* rushed into the passageway like a maddened herd of cattle. Then the outer door was flung open too, and it grew a little lighter in the loft. Rybak's unseeing eyes focussed once more on the black beam from which an old rusty sickle dangled in the straw. A few shadows thrown by the new light flickered and mingled with the shadow cast by the underside of the thatch.

'A ladder. Get a ladder!' A voice accustomed to command gave the order in a hoarse bass.

'There isn't a ladder, and there's no one up there. What are you going on about?' Demchikha started to cry again.

There was a banging, boots scraped on the plank wall, then quite close to them a breathless voice said:

'It's very dark in here. Can't see a thing.'

'What d'you mean, you can't see anything? Get in there, you mother-fucker.'

'Who's in here? Get out, or I'll throw a grenade in.' The voice sounded as if it was right up in the roof. But they hadn't yet heard any footsteps on the floor of the loft—the militia were evidently still trying to pluck up enough courage to come right in.

'You don't expect him to come out and give himself up!' bellowed the bass voice from below. 'Is there anywhere to hide up there?'

85

'Yes. It looks like hay.'

'Just poke through it with a bayonet, then.'

'I can't reach from here.'

'Oh, fuck your mother! What sort of soldier are you? Here, take this machine-gun and give them a burst!'

This is it. Full stop, thought Rybak. He had an almost physical sensation of his body being torn to pieces by a scorching burst of automatic fire. Trying to use his last seconds to the full, he cast around for an escape route, but could think of absolutely nothing. Everything was over, the only thing left was to stand-up; but he found that he wanted Sotnikov to be the first to stand. For a start he was wounded and ill, it was his coughing that had given them away, it was much more appropriate for him to give himself up. Sotnikov, however, lay like a corpse, contorted, his body stiff, as if he had already stopped breathing.

'So you're not going to give yourself up!'

There was a dry, metallic noise at the other end of the loft—the familiar sound of the safety-catch on an automatic being moved to the firing position. The next thing to happen would be the worst, after which nothing worse could possibly happen. Only a second or two separated them from the frontier between life and death, but even then Sotnikov didn't move a muscle, didn't even cough. Rybak couldn't stand it any longer. He thrust the flax away with his feet.

'Hands up!' yelled the militiaman.

Rybak got to his knees, scared that the militiaman might let off a burst at him by accident. He crawled on all fours away from the eaves and stood up. Peering over the beam at the entrance to the loft, he could see a motionless head in a fur hat gazing at him cautiously and a little fearfully. Beside the head the barrel of the automatic rifle pointed steadily at him. That barrel was the most frightening thing—it could decide everything. Looking at it steadily, but sideways, Rybak raised his hands. So far no one had fired, death had been put off again, that was the main thing, nothing else mattered.

'Ah, my doves, you've flown straight into the trap, you mother-fuckers.' The *politsai* made the curse sound almost like a kindly greeting. He climbed into the loft.

10

A ladder was produced from somewhere and all three climbed into the loft, rooted in the corners, shook up the flax, and picked up the rifles. While two of them searched, the prisoners stood over by the chimney with the third man holding them at machine-gun point.

Sotnikov took the weight off his bare foot, leant against the chimney and coughed. Now there was no need to hold it back, and he coughed as much as he wanted. Oddly enough he was not frightened of the *politsai*, nor of the thought that they might kill him—he was totally preoccupied by his own responsibility for what had happened. He thought in anguish of the harm he had caused Rybak and Demchikha. He deeply regretted that he had not killed himself while he still had a rifle, or that he had not died during the fight with the *politsai* on the hillside during the night—why need he have dragged himself here just to fall stupidly into their hands? He would rather have sunk into the ground than meet Demchikha now. She had every reason to tear out his and Rybak's eyes for having got her into this position. In his despair he knew there was no point in even challenging the *politsai* to shoot them—they would die, but only the two of them—Demchikha would be left alive to face whatever was to follow.

The *politsai* pushed them towards the ladder with curses and blows, and down into the passageway, where Demchikha was sobbing by the wide-open door into the cottage and the youngest child was howling in terror behind the partition. Rybak went down the ladder quickly, but Sotnikov took his time, using his hands alone, and the senior militia man, a broad-shouldered character with a grim, bandit's face, dressed in a black railway greatcoat, grabbed him by the shoulder so violently that he and the ladder fell off the millstones to the ground. He didn't land particularly heavily, just banged his leg hard again. His vision blurred, he caught his

87

breath and waited a moment before trying to drag himself wearily to his feet.

'What are you doing, you villains?' screamed Demchikha. 'Can't you see he's wounded, are you blind? Cannibals, all of you!'

The senior man turned authoritatively to the one in the fur hat. 'Stas!'

Stas obviously knew what was expected of him. He took the cleaning rod from his rifle and began to beat the woman's back.

'Swine,' shouted Sotnikov hoarsely, finally losing his self-control. 'What's that for? What's she done to deserve that?'

The outburst of anger seemed to restore some of his strength. He scrambled up until he was leaning against the wall, and shaking with rage turned to face Stas. At that moment it never crossed his mind that the shout might be his last, that the *politsai* might shoot him on the spot. But even if it had occurred to him, he would still have been unable to restrain himself from trying to defend the unfortunate Demchikha, towards whom he bore such a burden of guilt. But Stas, so quick on the uptake, clearly wasn't going to shoot just yet. He merely grinned unpleasantly, and returned the rod to his rifle with an accurate, precise movement.

'You'll find out what that's for.'

Sotnikov got himself a little more under control, got his breath back and began to calm down. Everything was perfectly plain. Since they hadn't shot them at once, that meant there would soon be interrogations and torture, which, of course, would end in death. There seemed no way out any more—all his hopes had come to nothing.

In the passageway they were searched, everything was taken from their pockets—their meagre provisions, their cartridges—their hands were tightly bound with leather straps, Rybak's behind him and Sotnikov's in front, and they were both made to sit on the rough earth floor. Then the senior militiaman went into the hut to see Demchikha, while the one they called Stas stayed on the threshold to guard them.

The freezing air in the passageway set Sotnikov's chest going again, his head began to spin sickeningly and his frozen ears tingled in the frost. He had lost his forage cap somewhere, probably in the loft, and now he sat with his tousled head bare. His wounded leg was freezing too, and hurt the more because of it. His knee had swollen, and he found it difficult to bend it. His bare foot had swollen, too, and had turned a blueish crimson. He could have asked someone to bring him his boot, but when he thought how painful it would be to try to get it on he decided, the hell with it. Now nothing made any difference—his foot could freeze until it dropped off, soon it would be no use to him anyhow. As he sat coughing on the floor, he had a look at the guard—a young lively lad in a stylish fur hat. Sometimes an unexpectedly attractive smile flitted across his handsome face with its well shaped nose. That smile made him look young and straightforward. You might have taken him for a young soldier—or that might merely have been his army jacket and regulation leather boots, into which, however, were tucked black civilian trousers. His rifle was slung on one shoulder, and the other was propped against the doorpost, where he stood looking up the street, spitting pumpkin-seeds on the ground, waiting for transport. But for the time being there was no transport, and after stamping up and down briefly he sat down on the doorstep with his rifle between his knees. From this short distance he examined Rybak and Sotnikov closely, but without hostility, rather as if he regarded them as something of a joke.

'Crawled under the flax, eh? Like cockroaches!'

They didn't reply, but Rybak, trying to make out what he really meant, glanced at him and then lowered his head again.

'So now they'll give you a real good scrubbing and then hang you out—that'll dry you off nicely.' He laughed so openly and naturally that Sotnikov caught himself thinking what a cheerful lad he was. But then the laughter broke off and in a completely different tone, which made them wince, the militiaman bawled at the top of his voice:

'You filthy bastards! You killed Khodoronok, didn't you? We'll unwind your guts for what you did to Khodoronok!'

'We've never heard of your Khodoronok,' said Rybak dully.

'Never heard of him, have you? Perhaps it wasn't you shooting last night?'

'It wasn't us.'

'Well, whether it was you or not, we'll break your ribs for you. Got it?'

Stas grew serious; his eyes turned cold and threatening; the human quality, the youthful decency disappeared from his face and was replaced by a hard, soulless determination.

There was a brief silence. Then perhaps merely to change the

89

subject, Rybak asked quietly:

'Have you been in the army?'

'Which army?'

'Let's say the Red Army.'

'I'd like to shit on your goddamned army, do you hear?' The militiaman burst out even more vehemently, his expressive eyes widening alarmingly. Then his face gradually changed again and softened, and the deceptive smile returned to his lips. He moved his leg to one side, and rubbed the sole of his boot on the earth floor of the passageway.

'What about the jacket, then?'

'Oh, the jacket. I got it off a commissar—a Jew, he was. He didn't need it any more,' the *politsai* replied, and added, in response to Rybak's questioning glance, 'We'll take your sheepskin as well. Budila will have it. It's his turn. That's the way it goes. Got it?'

'And it hasn't choked you yet?' Sotnikov said quietly, restraining himself with difficulty.

'What?'

'I said hasn't it choked you yet? The sheepskin coats and the rest of it?'

'Why should it choke us? We've got Germany behind us, got it, fool? As for you—*kaput*! You can be sure of that, sure as hell!' Stas ended harshly.

Well, that was straightforward enough. They could scarcely have expected anything else. Rybak sat dully, his head bowed, and Sotnikov, half-lying on his side, tried to move his leg—his thigh had stiffened, and the narrow rawhide strap was biting into his wrists.

Eventually the other *politsai* appeared with two sleighs. They left one in the street and brought the other right up to the door, its runners squealing and the harness jangling. Stas got up from the doorstep. First he pushed Rybak in, and then lifted Sotnikov from the ground with one powerful heave on his collar. Somehow or other Sotnikov reached the sleigh and fell onto the straw alongside Rybak. The militiaman got on to the back. The driver—a frightened old man in a ragged jacket—gingerly squeezed into the front. Sotnikov tucked his freezing bare foot under the skirts of his coat to try to ward off the pain. He was feeling rotten again, as though consciousness was slipping away. He pulled himself together with a great effort. The great need now was for patience, and so he waited, concentrating on economising his meagre resources of strength.

He expected that they would be on their way soon, but for some reason or other the senior *politsai* had not come back from the house, and the other one, the one who had brought the sleighs, went inside after him. Soon they heard voices, and Demchikha weeping. Sotnikov listened anxiously—were they going to leave her behind or not? For a moment it sounded as if they were looking for something in the house, the ladder banged against the cross-beam in the passageway, the children were sobbing, and then he heard Demchikha's desperate cry.

'What are you doing to me, you swine? May you die before Sunday! May you never see your own mothers again.'

'Come on now, quickly, I said. Get a move on.'

'Who can I leave the children with? You merciless bastards.'

'Get moving.'

No, they weren't leaving her—so their situation was even more difficult. And probably there'd be worse to come. Sotnikov looked at Rybak sitting sideways. Rybak's face, covered in thick stubble, was contorted in a grimace of suffering—and with good cause.

They came out on to the road along that same path by the fence and turned down past the graveyard. Sotnikov thrust his head deeper into the turned-up collar of his greatcoat and lightly rested his shoulder against Rybak's sheepskin back. He closed his eyes helplessly. The sleigh jerked along beneath them as the runners skidded across the ruts. He could hear Stas still spitting out his seeds. They were obviously being taken either to *politsai* headquarters or to the Gestapo—in other words, they didn't have much time of their own left, they should be gathering their strength and preparing for the worst. Of course, they wouldn't tell them the truth, although they couldn't very well conceal the fact that they'd come from the forest. The main thing was to protect Demchikha. Poor woman—hurrying home from work without the slightest idea of what was waiting for her! Now she was yelling her head off behind them, cursing and weeping, and the *politsai* with the hoarse voice was bawling back at her, in a flood of shameless obscenity. But Demchikha was giving as good as she got.

'Beasts! German dogs! Where are you taking me? The children are back there! My own children, my darlings! Oh, Galechka, how are you going to manage?'

'You should have thought of that before.'

'Oh, you rotten bastard! *You* reproach *me*, you damned

turncoat! What harm have I done you?'

'You hid the bandits.'

'It's you who are the bandits. They behaved like ordinary people, they just came in and went out. How was I to know they'd sneaked into the loft? What d'you take me for, an enemy to my own children? You're just filth! Fascists!'

'Shut up, or I'll have you gagged!'

'Oh, may you be impaled on a stake, you rotten bastard!'

'That's enough! Stas, stop!' Demchikha's guard shouted from the sleigh behind, and they pulled up just short of two slender birch saplings standing in the midst of a willow thicket over the ditch. Rybak and the driver turned round, but Sotnikov hunched himself in expectation of some new barbarity. Soon Demchikha screamed, struggling in the sleigh. The sleigh behind drove up closer—he could hear the yoke scraping and even the horse scuffling uneasily in the snow. Then everything went quiet. Stas had jumped out of their sleigh, but soon climbed back in, looking pleased with himself.

'A glove down her throat—that'll stop her yelling, the mad bitch!'

Sotnikov turned with enormous effort and found himself face to face with the guard.

'Murderers!'

'You make a fine protector for her! Turn round or I'll give you a bloody nose,' the *politsai* howled, his face twisted with rage. But Sotnikov knew the kind of man he was dealing with and ignored his threat.

'Just you try, you bastard.'

'Try, try! I could shoot you here and now and I wouldn't have to answer for it to anyone. You're not dealing with your Soviets now.'

'Go ahead and shoot.'

'You think I won't?'

The *politsai* grabbed the safety-catch of his rifle with a show of determination, but all he did was to thump Sotnikov in the chest with the butt and curse. Sotnikov didn't even gasp. He wasn't afraid of this renegade. The only answer to his bragging arrogance was a dose of the same medicine—people like that only understood when you spoke to them in their own language.

'Just you remember that the woman's nothing to do with all this,' he said, as a hint to Rybak as to how they should answer the interrogator's questions. 'We got into her loft without her

92

knowing.'

'You save your old wives' tales for old wives.' Stas wagged his head sagely and let go of his rifle. 'Budila will beat the nonsense out of you. You just wait.'

'We'd like to spit on your Budila.'

'You will pretty soon—but you'll be spitting blood.'

Why the hell is he trying to get him mad? thought Rybak angrily, as he listened to Sotnikov's slanging match.

They were being driven along the same road they had taken into the village that morning, but this time the countryside didn't look as open and tediously flat. They were going too quickly, and Rybak wanted desperately to slow the journey down. He felt in his heart that these were his last hours of relative freedom; soon they would have not even the slightest chance of escape. He cursed himself for his lack of forethought, for having been so stupid as to climb into that bloody loft, for not having avoided the last cottage in the village—he should have known better, the Germans always visited the end house. He could not forgive himself for having gone into the village so thoughtlessly—they would have been better off spending the day lying up in a thicket somewhere. Nothing had gone right from the very start of the mission. Even before they started no one would have given them good odds on success, but who could have dreamt that it would turn out like this.

And it was all Sotnikov's fault. Rybak had tried hard to suppress the anger he felt towards his companion, but now it could be restrained no longer. Rybak knew absolutely that had it not been for Sotnikov, for his cold, and then his wound, they would probably have got back to the forest. At all events, they wouldn't have been taken by the *politsai.* They had rifles and they could have defended themselves. But once they had let themselves be driven up into the loft of a cottage where there were children, a rifle wasn't much use.

Rybak swore briefly in anger, as he imagined vividly how eagerly their return was awaited in the forest, while the men were eating the last crumbs they could scrape from their pockets. They probably thought that he and Sotnikov were taking so long because they were driving a cow back with them. And, of course, they could have got a cow . . . Rybak had never let himself be taken before, because he had a sound head on his shoulders and on the whole was a good soldier.

93

Until he had come across Sotnikov.

He had first met Sotnikov by chance a week or ten days before when their group had broken out of the Borkovskiy forest and had to cross the main highway. They had been late. It had been daylight by the time they reached the road, and they had been spotted by a German transport column. The Germans opened fire, accelerated and began to chase them. In an attempt to get away, their commander had ordered three of them—himself, Sotnikov and another partisan called Gastinovich—to stay back to give covering fire. But how long could three men hold out against thirty or forty Germans with machine-guns? Very soon they began to be forced back, keeping up sporadic, rifle-fire, while the German fire increased in intensity. Rybak thought, that's my lot! To make matters worse, beyond the end of the wood which bordered the road lay an open stretch of snow-covered country with a clump of fir trees in the distance, towards which the tattered remains of the partisan group were making the best speed they could. It would be almost impossible to survive in open terrain like that under the fire of a couple of dozen Germans. Then Sotnikov yelled, 'Start running, I'll stay here!'

Rybak didn't need to be persuaded. He and Gastinovich, a rather slow-moving elderly local partisan, leapt to their feet and set off, zigzagging in short bursts towards the trees. Behind them Sotnikov started firing so accurately that several of the Germans were forced to flatten themselves in the snow. He had probably killed several Nazis by the time Rybak and Gastinovich reached a pile of stones which gave them enough cover to open fire themselves.

They kept up a lively fire from there for about five minutes, giving Sotnikov a chance of catching up with them. He managed to get across the most dangerous stretch despite the machine-gun fire, reached the stones, lay down beside them and waved them forward. It was a good thing that on that occasion at least they had enough ammunition. Sotnikov picked off another machine-gunner who had been a bit too eager, coming on ahead and spraying the countryside with tracer bullets. The others saw his mistake and slowed down. All the same one bullet found its mark in Gastinovich, who fell awkwardly in the snow and rolled on to his side. Immediately Sotnikov dashed to him, but he was past any help. Sotnikov grabbed his rifle and managed to rejoin Rybak.

The two of them lay behind a low hillock. It was safer there;

94

when they had got their breath back they would be able to run on. But suddenly Rybak remembered that Gastinovich had a hunk of bread in his haversack which he had got hold of the previous night at a farmhouse. They had been starving for a week; the bread weighed so heavily on Rybak's mind that after a brief hesitation he crawled back to the dead man. Sotnikov moved higher up the hillock and opened fire on the Germans again, covering Rybak, who managed to cross the hundred yards or so to Gastonovich's body. They divided the bread immediately and ate it before catching up with the rest of the group.

Then everything quietened down again, the group bivouacked in the Gorely swamp, and he and Sotnikov, although they still only knew one another slightly, began to go around together. They slept side by side, and shared a mess-tin. It might have been because of that that they had found themselves selected for this mission.

But now they'd reached the end of the road, that was clear. It didn't matter much that they hadn't tried to shoot it out—they'd been taken with their rifles and that was enough to get them both shot. Of course Rybak hadn't expected anything else when he got up from behind the heap of flax, but all the same . . .

He wanted to live. He had still not lost all hope; any second there might be a chance of dodging fate and getting away. Sotnikov was no longer his responsibility now they had been captured. If Rybak had a chance to escape, his conscience would be clear—in these circumstances there was no possibility of saving a wounded man. He had kept his eyes open ever since he had had to put his hands up—in the loft; in the passageway he had been on the look-out for a loophole of escape. But there had been no chance, and now his hands were tied—no matter how he turned and twisted them, the strap showed no signs of yielding. And he cursed the strap—the strap which might be holding him back from his last chance of escape.

Perhaps it would be worth trying his luck even with his hands tied? But if he were to do so, he would need a more suitable place, somewhere not so flat, a turn in the road maybe, or a steep valley with bushes at the bottom, a sharp dip, or some trees. Unfortunately here it was all flat and open. The road climbed a hillside and then began to go down into a shallow valley. At one point they crossed a bridge, but the valley beneath it was very shallow and open, with nowhere to hide. Rybak kept as sharp a watch as he could without twisting his head too much, trying to find a place which offered some chance of flight, and found nothing.

As time passed, and they came nearer to the small town, the greater Rybak's alarm—almost total despair—grew. It became more and more indisputable—they had had it.

I I

Sotnikov had never for a moment doubted that they had had it. He had no intention of trying to escape, nor had he any hope of mercy at the hands of the *politsai*. He maintained a tense silence, depressed by the weight of the guilt which lay on him for two reasons—Rybak and Demchikha. He was especially concerned about Demchikha. But for the moment he didn't know what the *politsai* knew about her and how seriously they suspected her of having connections with the partisans. And he thought of the shooting the previous night, when apparently one of the bastards had got shot, someone called Khodoronok. Of course, Sotnikov had shot him, but neither Rybak nor even more so Demchikha had anything to do with it.

They were driving into the town. The road was tree-lined—for some way it passed between two ranks of willows, and then turned into a paved street. It was fairly late in the day now, but there was still some smoke curling from chimneys as if the people inside were only just lighting their stoves, and a cold winter sun hung over the frosted roofs in a bitter winter mist. Ahead of them a woman hurried across the street with a yoke on her shoulders. She turned to go into a house, and glanced back in muted terror at the sleigh and the *politsai*. In a yard opposite, a lank-haired girl wearing galoshes was throwing slops on to the snow. And before she turned back fearfully into the house, she too peered curiously at the road. Somewhere a dog howled briefly. The sparrows huddled uncomfortably in the branches of the willow. Life was going on—uneasy, difficult, but at all events normal life which Rybak and Sotnikov had not known for so long and now would never know again.

The sleigh crossed a bridge and turned off into a side alley near a two-storied wooden house. Apparently they had arrived. Oddly enough Sotnikov was anxious for them to get where they were going—the cold wind in the field had been bitter and freezing.

Human habitation offered, as always, warmth and shelter, although on this occasion, of course, the shelter available held out no hope of any pleasure. Still, he longed to get inside any building, just to get warm—and then . . . Well, then, let whatever was going to happen happen.

In the distance Sotnikov made out a wide gateway with a *politsai* standing by it in an ankle-length coat, a rifle tucked under his arm. Beyond the gates there was a solid stone-built house, which had probably been a shop or an office building, with four barred windows in the facade. When they drew closer, the grim-looking guard slung his rifle on his shoulder and opened the gates. The sleigh drove into the large yard, the surface of the snow carefully swept and levelled, with an old battered horse trough by the fence and a sort of shed with a wooden latrine in the corner. Another *politsai* came out on to the steps of the house, a small, smartly turned-out man in a German tunic, with a carefully ironed white armband on his sleeve.

'Brought them in, have you?'

'Of course we have!' replied Stas, proudly. 'Didn't you expect us to? Here you are, take charge of the bastards.'

He jumped lightly from the sleigh, his automatic rifle slung casually on his shoulder—there was a fence all round the yard with no chance of escape. While the driver and Rybak climbed out of the sleigh, Sotnikov looked dully at the house, where in all probability they were going to discover just what pain and evil were. There were solid walls, a high porch with a metal roof, and some steps leading down to a door in the basement. One of the barred windows had plywood instead of glass, with some traces of writing in German gothic script. Everything was spick and span, and you could feel the discipline and strength of this nest of *politsai*, this fortress of German power. The *politsai* in the tunic took a key from his pocket and went down the steps to the basement door, which was secured by a heavy padlock and a metal bar.

'Get them all down here!'

They had all got out of the sleighs—Stas, Rybak and the driver. A little way off, the *politsai* were stamping their feet and shaking out their greatcoats, and Demchikha was standing despairingly. The sight of her clutched painfully at Sotnikov. She stood hunched, her hands tied. Her headscarf had slipped down to her shoulders, and a cloth glove stuck ridiculously out of her mouth—obviously they

98

were in no hurry to remove the gag.

Sotnikov didn't find it easy to get out of the sleigh—whichever way he turned, a searing pain ran through his leg. He mastered the pain enough to slide out on to the snow, and hopped a couple of steps near the sleigh. He was waiting for Demchikha, and when she got close to him, deliberately avoiding his eyes, he raised his bound hands and removed the gag.

'What are you doing? What's that for, you swine?' bellowed a *politsai* from behind him, and the next moment a powerful blow from a boot stretched him on the ground.

The pain in his leg spread to his whole body. For a moment he couldn't even see. He gritted his teeth without a word, but he was neither surprised nor angered by the kick—he accepted it as something he deserved. Then he burst out in a coughing fit and slowly began to get up, as the senior *politsai* bellowed menacingly, 'Oh, you communist bastard! What a marvellous protector she's got! Stas, get him into the cells! Get him to Budila!'

And then behind him Demchikha burst out, showering curses on Hitler, and they all turned on her in a frenzy of rage. Their anger and their harsh curses showed a frightening intensity of hate for their captives, which they now displayed in full measure.

When he had silenced Demchikha, the agile diligent Stas hurried over to Sotnikov and grabbed him violently by the arm. Sotnikov again fell to the ground, his bound hands stretched before him, but the young *politsai* heaved him up again unceremoniously by sheer brute strength and dragged him up the steps, over the threshold and through the door. In trying to protect his injured leg, Sotnikov crashed his shoulder heavily against the door post. Stas dragged him along the corridor, kicked open one of the doors and hurled Sotnikov on to the trampled, wet floor. As a sign of farewell he let off a volley of curses and slammed the door behind him.

It was suddenly quiet. The only sounds were steps in the corridor, and from the next room he could hear the muffled tones of a measured voice, apparently reading something aloud. Sotnikov struggled to overcome the vicious pain in his leg. Slowly he raised his face. There was no one else in the room, which puzzled him a little, and with a sudden hope he looked at the window, but it was firmly protected by iron bars. No, there was no way out there! When he realised this, he lay back on the floor, glancing round the room with no great interest. It seemed a normal kind of office, uncomfortable and sparsely furnished, despite the grey baize-covered table with an ancient sagging armchair behind the table, and a rickety upright chair near the tiled stove, whose round black sides radiated a heavy, very pleasant warmth. But a cold draught poured into the room from under the door. Sotnikov shivered with fever, and carefully stretched his leg to one side, holding back the groan which rose in his throat.

Well, this is where it's all going to end, he thought. God, if only I can hold out! He had reached his limit, his ultimate breaking point. He had come close to it many times during the war, but this time he had almost no strength left. Yet the only thing he was afraid of was that he might not be able to hold out physically, that he might cave in despite himself. As he breathed in the warm air, he began to cough, getting the usual convulsive spasms in his chest and a hammering in his brain. It was the same importunate persistent cough, which had tormented him for the last two days. He hadn't coughed like this since his childhood, when his colds had worried his mother so much, and she had been so anxious about his weak lungs. But his coughs and colds had never been serious, he had grown out of them, and had lived more or less free of sickness up to the present, at twenty-six years of age. And now—well, now, his health wasn't of all that much importance any more.

Because he was coughing, he didn't hear someone come into the room. Suddenly on the floor in front of his face there appeared a pair of shoes, not new, but well cared for, with well repaired toe caps, and polished uppers. Sotnikov raised his head.

Opposite him stood an elderly man wearing a dark civilian jacket with a tie knotted over a grubby pale striped shirt, and serge breeches of a military cut. His small penetrating eyes showed a certain calm authority, and a degree of reasonableness. A small moustache, like Hitler's, grew under his nose. Can this be Budila? Sotnikov thought doubtfully, although this man didn't appear to have any of the bestial characteristics which the *politsai* ascribed to Budila. Yet he gave the impression of being in command, and Sotnikov sat a little more upright, as far as the pain in his leg would let him.

'Who did this to you? Gamanyuk?' asked the man, in a quiet, authoritative voice.

'Your Stas,' said Sotnikov in a voice which held an unexpected note of complaint. He immediately regretted that he had not

100

maintained a neutral tone. The man abruptly opened the door to the corridor.

'Gamanyuk! Come here!'

His cough began to die down, leaving only weakness and pain. It was very uncomfortable trying to prop himself up on the floor with his hands tied. Sotnikov suffered, but remained silent, puzzled at the man's seemingly protective intervention. In half a minute or so Stas hurried into the room and with marked servility clicked the heels of his smart boots.

'Yes, sir?'

The older man frowned, wrinkling his high-domed forehead, which seemed a little too large for his small, lined face.

'What's going on? Why this brutality again? Why on the floor? Why didn't you tell me he was here?'

'I'm sorry,' Stas pulled his elbows in and stood even more rigidly to attention.

But the unthinking way he did so, and the emotionless severity of his superior, immediately made Sotnikov suspect that all this was nothing more than an ill-conceived and ill-played farce, aimed at fooling him.

'Have you ever been ordered to behave like this? It isn't the German command who've taught you to do this kind of thing, is it?' He didn't pause for a reply, rapping his questions out at the *politsai,* who stood in simulated fear, thrusting out his chest even further.

'I'm sorry. I won't do it again! I'm sorry!'

'The German authorities guarantee prisoners appropriate treatment, which I would describe as humane treatment . . .'

Really, that was enough! Sotnikov was already aware of how the German authorities treated their prisoners, and hesitated no longer in interrupting this ridiculous play-acting.

'You're wasting your time!'

The senior policeman turned sharply to him, pretending that he had not heard, his brow wrinkling in mock concern.

'What did you say?'

'You heard. Untie my hands. I can't sit like this!'

The policeman hesitated, scowling. Then he seemed to decide that there was nothing to be afraid of, thrust his hand into his pocket and produced a knife. He inserted the tip of the blade in the knot of the strap, cut through it with a single stroke, and put the knife away. Sotnikov chafed his swollen wrists where the straps had left a weal.

'Anything else?'

'A drink,' said Sotnikov. He had decided to try to quench his thirst while there was still a chance, so as to be able to hold out later.

The policeman nodded to Gamanyuk.

'Get some water!'

Stas hurried into the corridor while the policeman walked round the table and sat down comfortably in his chair. Throughout the whole scene he had behaved in a restrained and cautious manner, as if he were concealing something very important and promising for the prisoner. His sharp, somehow anxious eyes hardly left Sotnikov's face.

'You can sit in that chair.'

Sotnikov got up from the floor as best he could and let himself drop sideways into the chair, leaving his leg out at one side. That felt more comfortable, he could hold out better like that. He breathed heavily, gazed round the walls, looked behind the stove, into the corner by the window, without immediately realising that he was looking for some instruments of torture—surely there should be something of that kind here. But to his surprise he couldn't see anything that looked as if it would serve. At the same time he felt that his relations with this policeman had already exceeded the bounds of convention, and that, now that the trick had failed, the real interrogation—which promised nothing good—was about to begin.

Stas Gamanyuk brought in an enamel jug of water, and Sotnikov drained it thirstily. The policeman at the table waited patiently, watching every movement, apparently considering something, or possible trying to understand something.

'Well, let's get to know each other,' he said pleasantly enough, when Stas had left the room. 'My name is Portnov. Police investigator.'

'Mine wouldn't mean anything to you.'

'All the same . . .'

'Well, let's say Ivanov,' said Sotnikov through his teeth. His leg was hurting.

'I've no objection. Ivanov, so be it. That's what we'll write down,' said the interrogator, although he wrote nothing. 'What detachment are you in?'

Oho, detachments already! Before attempting to answer this

extremely difficult and unpleasant question, Sotnikov was silent for a moment. The interrogator, his eyes boring like gimlets into Sotnikov's face, picked up an ink-stained wooden paper-weight from the table, and turned it in his fingers. Sotnikov looked unseeingly at the interrogator's hands, and wondered what was the best course—to pretend to spill the beans, or to refuse to answer so as to avoid being drawn into lies and confusion. The more so as this man would probably not believe his lies.

'Do you expect that I'll tell you the truth?'

'Oh, you will, you will,' said the interrogator, quietly but with such total conviction that Sotnikov for a second lost control, and looked sharply up from under his brows at the policeman's face. 'You'll tell the truth in the end!'

That was a very unpromising start. Of course he wouldn't answer that question, but the others wouldn't be any easier. The interrogator waited, abstractly playing with the paper-weight. The movements of his long thin fingers were relaxed and confident, but Sotnikov was aware of a concealed tension beneath the composed exterior. It was strange how in appearance he looked so unlike the typical interrogator-executioner with a good many butcheries to his credit, far more like a humble, shabby country clerk. But at the same time Sotnikov was aware of something treacherous, per-fidious, slumbering beneath the surface, threatening the prisoner at every moment. Sotnikov settled down to await the moment when it would break out—although he could not work out how strong this man's nerves were, and which answer would finally make him blow his top.

'What mission were you on? Where were you going? How long has this woman been your agent?'

'She's not an agent at all. We picked on her cottage by chance and hid in the loft. She wasn't even home at the time,' Sotnikov explained calmly.

'By chance, of course, yes. That's what they all say. And you dropped in on the headman of Lyesiny by chance as well, I suppose?'

So that's the way it was! So they already knew about the headman. Although of course he'd probably reported them that evening. Just wanted to keep his nose clean, not to get involved. But that meant that the *politsai* had known about them long before they had realised, and Sotnikov was confused for a moment.

Probably that was a deliberate trap in the interrogation.

The interrogator noticed the effect he had achieved, threw the paper-weight back on to the table and lit a cigarette. Then he tidily picked up his cigarette case and lighter from the table, brushed the scraps of tobacco to the floor, and watched Sotnikov through smoke, waiting for an answer.

'Yes, it was by chance,' said Sotnikov firmly after a pause.

'That's not very original. You're an intelligent man, and yet you're hoping to get out of it by primitive lies like that. You won't fool us that way.'

Won't fool them—probably not. But the hell with them! As if he'd hoped to get away with it. He no longer hoped for anything at all, he just felt sorry for the unfortunate Demchikha, and couldn't think of any way of getting her out of it.

'You can deal with us just as you think fit,' said Sotnikov as calmly and reasonably as he could manage, 'but please don't do anything to the woman. It was just that her cottage was the nearest, and I couldn't walk any further.'

'Where were you wounded?'

'In the leg.'

'I don't mean that. Where, in what area?'

'In the forest, two days ago.'

'That won't do,' said the interrogator, looking steadily at him. 'Spill it. It wasn't in the forest, it was on the road, last night.'

Hell, does he know, or is he trying to trap me? thought Sotnikov. He didn't know the best way to carry on. If he lied badly about small things, they wouldn't believe him even when he was speaking the truth. And it was very important to him to convince the interrogator of the truth about Demchikha, although he felt that was going to be more difficult than getting away with a downright lie. The situation was developing as badly as it possibly could.

'And if I admit that, will you let the woman go? Can you promise me that?'

The interrogator's eyes suddenly flashed with anger, and seemed to pierce right through him.

'I'm not going to promise you a thing! I'll ask the questions, and you'll answer them.'

In other words, that won't work, Sotnikov thought dully. Of course he can't let anyone get away. It's a well known custom. So Demchikha had probably had it as well.

'There's no call to kill the woman. She's got three children.'

'We're not killing her. You are! It was you who dragged her into your band! Why didn't you think about the children then?' snapped the interrogator. 'It's too late now. Do you know the laws of Great Germany?'

Laws! thought Sotnikov, it can't be all that long since you learnt them yourself, you bloody traitor. Not all that long ago you were probably chewing over quite different laws! Yet the interrogator's last question sounded a little like double meaning, as if he wouldn't have minded shuffling something off his own shoulders on to those of 'Great Germany'.

Sotnikov remained silent. The interrogator rose from behind the table, pushed the chair away, and crossed to the window. He stared absently out through the bars into the yard, from where Sotnikov could hear the voices of the *politsai*. Again the interrogator gave the impression of concealing something. He wasn't pressing on with the interrogation, and seemed either to be working out some new trap, or thinking about something personal, something nothing to do with the questioning.

There were heavy footsteps in the corridor, followed by voices and cursing. It sounded as if someone was being dragged along or carried out of the building. When the commotion had passed by out on to the porch, the interrogator turned back and said forcefully:

'Right. We've had enough playing hide and seek! Tell me your detachment, the names of its officers, means of communication, number of men, where it's based. And don't try to lie. You'll be wasting your time.'

'You're not asking much of me, are you?'

Unconsciously he was gradually falling back on sarcasm, as he usually did when he was obliged to speak to fools and rogues. Of course, for Stas or for the rest of the traitors like him, his irony would have been beyond comprehension, but it worked perfectly on this more senior figure. Yet up till now Portnov had managed to restrain himself with nothing more than an occasional tightening of his lips.

'Where were you going?'

'We had got lost.'

'That's not good enough. It's a lie! I'll give you two minutes to think.'

'Don't worry. You've probably got a lot of work to get through.'

That seemed to be a good guess. The wrinkled face of the interrogator twisted again, but he seemed to know how to control his feelings. He didn't even raise his voice.

'Do you want to live?'

'And if I do? Are you going to let me off?'

The interrogator creased up his eyes and looked out of the window.

'No, we aren't going to show you any mercy. We don't pardon bandits,' he said, and suddenly turned back from the window. The ash from his cigarette fell and broke on the toe of his shoe. It seemed that his patience had been tried enough. 'We're going to shoot you, make no mistake about that. But before we get that far, we're going to make mince-meat of you. We'll cut your body into little pieces. We'll pull your guts out, slowly. We'll break every bone in your body, one by one. And then we'll let it be known that you betrayed the others, just so that they won't pity you too much, out there in the forest.'

'You'll have to wait a long time. I shan't betray anyone.'

'If you don't, the other one will. And we'll put it all down to you. Got it? How d'you like that idea?'

Sotnikov felt dreadful, and he didn't reply. His face was covered in sweat, and any inclination towards sarcasm left him. He realised that this was no empty threat, no blackmail—they were capable of anything. Hitler had atrophied their consciences, their humanity and even their elementary human decency, and naturally their bestial strength was the greater for it. And in face of all that, Sotnikov was nothing but an ordinary man. He was responsible to his people and his country, and there wasn't much time left to explain or justify his actions. It was clear that in this war the weapons were not evenly balanced, and the enemy had the advantage. Everything that Sotnikov put forward was easy for the interrogator to throw back at him.

Portnov straddled his legs in the baggy-kneed breeches, looked long and sharply at Sotnikov with unconcealed scorn in his eyes, and waited. Sotnikov found himself in a tremendously difficult position, he felt himself slipping into unconsciousness, pouring with cold sweat. It was agonising trying to choose the words for his answer, and he felt that they might be his last words. The interrogator slowly stretched out his right hand towards the paper-weight on the table.

'Well?'

'Bastards!' was the only reply that Sotnikov could squeeze out.

A little more abruptly than was necessary, the interrogator grabbed the paper-weight and banged it down on the table, as if he were putting the final full stop on this bloodless, yet frightening interrogation.

'Send Budila in here!'

In the corridor there was a shout of 'Budila to the interrogator!' Then Portnov walked round the table and sat down calmly in his chair. He was no longer looking at Sotnikov—who seemed to have ceased to exist for him. He lit another cigarette. He'd finished his part of the job, and now they were up to the second part of the interrogation.

Sotnikov tried to remain outwardly calm, but inside he was tense when the door opened, revealing Budila standing on the threshold.

Probably he was the local police torturer and executioner—a powerful, buffalo-like young man with a bony face, something resembling a horse's. The fierce expression on his stupid face was unpleasant enough, but the most alarming thing about him was his huge hairy hands which protruded from his sleeves, looking as if they could bend horseshoes straight. As he came in, he fixed his victim—probably in accordance with usual procedure—with a threatening stare from his slightly squinting eyes.

'Well then.'

Overcome with fatigue, Sotnikov remained sitting, as if he were trying to thrust something unspeakably unpleasant away from him. Budila stepped over to the chair with a significant lack of haste. His huge hand reached out towards Sotnikov's sunken chest, grabbed the lapels of his greatcoat, tensed, and ripped him from the chair.

'Right then, bolshevist filth!'

12

'Well, that's it,' thought Rybak almost indifferently, when Stas grabbed Sotnikov in the yard and dragged him off into the building. He expected that he and Demchikha would be hauled in the same direction, but for them the *politsai* opened the door to the basement. Before they were pushed down the steps, they untied his hands and ripped the belt from his trousers. Demchikha's hands were left bound and the gag stuffed in her mouth again.

'Get down! Quickly!'

Down in the cellar it was pitch black, or perhaps it just seemed so to Rybak coming in from the daylight outside. At first they were in a kind of damp corridor. The *politsai* in front rattled an iron bolt, and Rybak bumped into Demchikha's back and stood still trying to ease life back into his numbed wrists.

'Get on, get on. Why have you stopped?' The *politsai* behind gave him a shove—apparently the door ahead of them had been opened. There was nothing to be done. Rybak slipped between Demchikha and the *politsai*, ducked his head cautiously and sensed that he was on the threshold of a stuffy dark little room. For a moment he could make nothing out at all, although there was a little light thrown on the ceiling from a small window set high in the wall. Below it was dark. There was a sour, stale smell of air, quite unfit to breathe, and he stood for a moment not knowing where to go next.

As he stood there the bolt went home behind him, and Demchikha stayed outside with the *politsai*, who took her further on. From the cell Rybak could hear their swift businesslike conversation.

'Where are we putting the woman? In the corner cell?'

'Yes, that'll do.'

'It's empty today, is it?'

'The Germans took a load away yesterday. There's only one

Jewess left.'

As he grew more accustomed to the darkness, Rybak made out the figure of a man in the corner. He was apparently totally absorbed in what he was doing, wriggling about in the darkness, either undressing or tucking his clothes beneath him, probably preparing for sleep. The dense darkness by the wall completely concealed the place where he was lying, and only his grey head and his shoulders could occasionally be glimpsed in the meagre light filtering through the window.

'Sit down. Why stand? There's nothing to stand for now.'

Rybak was surprised, and in a way cheered—the old man's voice seemed familiar, and then he remembered—the headman! And so it was—the man in the corner was their recent acquaintance, the headman Pyotr from the village of Lyesiny.

'You here as well?' Rybak burst out in astonishment.

'That's the way it turned out. They recognised the sheep, and so . . .'

'I see.' Now everything was clear. Oddly he had forgotten all about that damned sheep, and only now did it cross his mind, unforgivably late, just what harm it might bring on its owner.

'Still, why are you here? We robbed you of the sheep,' Rybak made his voice show more surprise than he really felt.

The headman tucked some piece of clothing beneath him, but did not lie down. He stayed sitting, leaning against the wall, almost completely hidden in the darkness. The weak light from the window fell on his knees alone.

'Well, how can you tell? If I'd been robbed, then I ought to have reported it . . . But I . . . It makes no difference now.'

It really did seem to make no difference, it was too late to get out of it, thought Rybak. Probably the *politsai* had known the whole story for some time.

He didn't bother to unfasten his coat, but lowered himself wearily to the straw-strewn litter on the floor, and leant his back against the wall. He couldn't think what to do next, but then there was nothing to do but wait. For the first time he realised just how exhausted he was, and began to drift off to sleep, but his thoughts kept running frighteningly round his head. Suddenly it crossed his mind that it might be a good idea to try to persuade the headman to say that it hadn't been him and Sotnikov who had stolen his sheep. It couldn't make things any the worse for the headman and it might conceivably make it easier for them to talk their way out of things. Rybak didn't feel at all guilty about Pyotr. After all it wasn't the first time he'd had to use methods like that to get food. And they'd only taken the one sheep, and that hadn't been from a decent, loyal family, but from a German-appointed headman. Rybak's conscience was entirely clear on this point. The only thing he found at all puzzling was why the headman had not put all the blame on them, so as to keep himself out of this stinking cellar.

An hour or more passed. Sotnikov did not appear, and Rybak caught himself wondering, not without a brief moment of sympathy, whether they had killed him. He didn't want to talk about anything. He felt that they would soon be coming for him, and that the worst part was about to begin. He kept turning things over in his mind, trying to find some way of outwitting the *politsai*, either to get himself off the hook altogether, or at least to postpone sentence. It seemed to him that there was only one way of doing that—to make the enquiry go on for a long time. (There must at least be some kind of investigation.) But to get them to do that he would have to tell them something new, something that would interest them, for if they decided that it was all cut and dried they wouldn't hang on to them for long. And that would be the final and definitive end.

It was quiet and drowsy in the cellar, the silence broken only by the sound of voices and footsteps from the floor above. Sometimes the noise got quite loud, there would be a muted sound of knocking, and a shouting voice could be clearly heard. All this bustling around upstairs could hardly fail to remind him of Sotnikov, and a feeling of anguished pity gripped his heart—poor, unlucky Sotnikov! But it seemed that he faced a similar fate. True, he didn't want to think about that—he was trying to sort out how to get out of the mess, and possibly even help Sotnikov out of it as well. But it looked as if there wasn't much chance of that. A gloomy twilight filtered through the small window, casting a dim patch of light on the trodden straw or occasionally illuminating the bent head of the headman, who sat motionless by the wall, enveloped in his own probably not very cheerful thoughts—now was a time for every man to examine his own feelings.

'They were saying that someone wounded one of the *politsai* last night,' the old man said after a long silence. 'They don't know yet whether he'll live.'

110

This was not news to Rybak, but it reminded him of the shooting and he grew even more alarmed. But he changed the subject.

'Have they taken you upstairs yet?' he asked, in the timid hope that it might not yet be his turn for interrogation. But the headman destroyed that hope immediately.

'For questioning? Yes, they have! Portnov interrogated me himself.'

'Who's Portnov?'

'Their investigator.'

'How was it? Did they beat you up?'

'They didn't beat me up. Why should they? They only do that to people who try to hide something. And what have I got to hide?'

Rybak held his breath and listened; he wanted to find out as much as he could about what he was going to have to face.

'That Portnov's a crafty one, crafty as the devil. He knows everything,' the old man said in a tone that made Rybak feel there was no hope left at all.

'You've got out of it all right.'

'Well, why shouldn't I get out of it? I'm not guilty of anything. Neither before God nor man.'

'As sinless as that?'

'Well, where have I sinned? Because I didn't rush off to tell them about the sheep? I'm a bit old for dashing about the place at nights. I'm sixty-seven.'

'Yes,' sighed Rybak, 'It's just a trumped up charge they've got you on. That's easy enough to do. Aid and comfort to partisans.'

In the same disinterested voice, Pyotr said, 'Well, that's fate. Nothing to be done . . .'

What humility, thought Rybak. At sixty-seven the headman had had his fair share anyway. But he was only twenty-six, and he wanted a bit more life on earth. It wasn't so much frightening as downright unpleasant to be buried in winter in the frozen ground.

No, he must fight!

How would it be if he were to get the headman involved much more deeply in the affair? If, for instance, he were to say that Pyotr was a partisan agent or a known sympathiser and helper and that this was far from being the first time he'd aided the group, perhaps that might turn the questioning on to a false course? They'd have to begin a new investigation, see new witnesses, take more depostions, and time would pass. It probably wouldn't increase Pyotr's guilt in the eyes of the Germans, and it might possibly help the two of them.

Sunk in his own thoughts, he suddenly started with surprise. There was a quiet rustling in the straw beside him, and something alive and soft scuttered across his feet. The headman in the corner moved his leg in disgust.

'Get the hell out of it, you filthy beast,' he said, and in the dim light from the window Rybak spotted the rat. Its agile swift-moving body with the long tail dragging behind scampered along the foot of the wall and disappeared in the dark corner.

'They breed here,' Pyotr said. 'They aren't afraid of people at all—carry on as if they were the bosses. It looks to me as if they're the same ones that were here when Itska had the place—it used to be a shop, and Itska sold sweets. Then it was the village store. Times change, but the rats keep on running about just the same.'

'Well, no one's trying to stop them here.'

'Yes, who's going to be bothered trying to catch a rat these days? Men are hunting for men—no time for rats. Oh, my God, what times we live in . . .'

He was interrupted by the sound of footsteps outside the door, and the familiar sound of the bolt. Their eyes were momentarily blinded by the brightness of the winter daylight. The lean figure of Stas appeared in the doorway in his belted army tunic, with a rifle slung over his shoulder.

'Where's the other bandit? To the interrogator!'

The *politsai* chuckled briefly and unpleasantly, and Rybak felt his guts turn over. He got to his feet a shade too quickly and went towards the door. Amid his ridiculous fear he wondered where Sotnikov was. They should have brought Sotnikov down to the cell first before they took him away for questioning. Or perhaps Sotnikov had already been killed.

He went obediently to the steps, waited for Stas to close the door behind him, and then climbed the stairs quickly ahead of his escort. He moved almost mechanically, unaware of what he was doing or of his surroundings. He felt terrible. It wasn't only fear—he was at his wit's end because there was nothing he could do to resist what was happening to him. All he knew about was how to fight and with that possibility removed he couldn't think which way to turn. The idea he had had about involving the headman was no more than a shapeless intention—he hadn't thought it out as he should have

112

done, hadn't come to any firm decision, and now he was on his way to interrogation in a state of total confusion.

'We'll have that sheepskin off you.' Stas clapped him heavily on the shoulder. 'It's not a bad coat, either, thank god. And your boots! I'll have the boots myself. It'd be a pity to wear these ones out, wouldn't it?', he said confidingly, waving in front of Rybak a foot clad in good calf leather. 'What size d'you take?'

'39,' lied Rybak, slowing his pace. After the musty cellar he wanted at least a chance to breathe a little.

'Goddamn, they're too small! I'll bust you in the mouth for that!' The *politsai* had suddenly turned nasty again. 'Get a move on.'

Fearing a blow, Rybak didn't try to resist. He jumped briskly up the porch steps, hurried through the door and down the short dark corridor, with a long-faced orderly sitting at a small table. Stas knocked politely at one of the doors with a crooked forefinger.

'May we come in?'

As if in a dream, with a premonition that he was now coming to the ultimate destruction of his entire, largely unsuccessful life, Rybak stepped across the threshold. The first thing he saw, standing across his path like some evil omen, was the huge stove, its black-tiled sides making it look a little like a hideous obelisk on a grave. Behind the table by the window stood a smallish man in a jacket, waiting. Rybak stopped by the door, wondering whether this could be the police investigator the headman had spoken of.

'Name?', the man rapped out. He was obviously angry about something; his elderly face was wrinkled threateningly, and he looked out at the prisoner from beneath lowered brows.

'Rybak,' answered the prisoner, wondering what came next.

'Born?'

'1916.'

'Where?'

'Near Gomel.'

The interrogator came away from the window and sat down at the table. He seemed to be on his guard, alert, but perhaps not as threatening as Rybak at first thought.

'Sit down.'

Rybak walked three paces and cautiously sat down on the squeaky upright chair by the table.

'Do you want to live?'

113

This strange question was so unexpected that it somehow lowered the tension. Rybak even thought he could detect something of a joke in it, and he shifted uneasily on the chair.

'Well, who doesn't want to live? Of course I do.'

But it seemed that the interrogator was not joking at all. He continued to shoot questions at Rybak.

'Right. Where were you going?'

The rapidity with which the questions were put probably implied a need for a similar rapidity in the replies, but Rybak was afraid of missing some trick in the interrogator's words, and paused fractionally before he replied.

'We were going for food. We had to bring our stocks up,' he said, and thought, the hell with him. Everyone knows that even partisans have to eat. There's no need to make a secret of that.

'Right. I'll accept that. Where were you going?'

He could see the interrogator tensing himself a little, watching for any change of expression on the prisoner's face. But Rybak smoothed his coat over his knee, and scratched at a stain on the skin. He was trying to think before he answered.

'Well, we were making for a farm, but it turned out to have been burnt down. So we just followed our eyes . . .'

'What farm was it that had been burnt?'

'Well, Kulgai's, is it? Is that the name? The one near the forest?'

'That's right. Kulgai's farm has been burnt down. The Germans did it. And Kulgai and all his family were shot.'

Rybak thought with relief, Thank God, that's one crime we needn't feel any guilt for.

'How did you come to be in Lyesiny?'

'It just turned out that way. We came across the village in the night, and went to see the headman . . .'

'I see.' The interrogator nodded, as if he were considering something. 'So you'd set out to see the headman?'

'No, why should we? We were going to the farm, like I told you.'

'To the farm, I see. And who's the commander of your group?', the interrogator asked suddenly, and sat very still, attentively, fixing Rybak with his piercing, all-seeing eyes. Rybak considered for a moment, and decided that he might try a lie here—let them try to check it. Unless Sotnikov . . .

'The commander of the group? Well, it's . . . Dubovoi.'

'Dubovoi?'—for some reason the interrogator seemed surprised, and Rybak looked him steadily in the eye. Not merely because he wanted to convince him that his lie was truth, but because it was important to know whether he was being believed or not.

'The bastard! We've already had a smell at Dubovoi. I knew it! We didn't pick him up in the autumn, and now . . .'

Rybak didn't understand; who did he mean? The headman? But if so, why? It looked as if he'd got mixed up at this point. But he didn't have time to think about it. Portnov hurried on with the questioning.

'Where is your group?'

'In the forest.'

Now he was answering without the slightest hesitation, looking directly and innocently into the coldly cautious eyes of the interrogator—he must make him believe in his absolute truthfulness.

'In the Borkovskiy forest?'

'Yes.'

(They were fools anyway to stay in the Borkovskiy forest. Although it was big it had been surrounded on four sides since the Islyanka bridge had been blown up. It was true enough that Dubovoi's group had stayed there, while the remains of their own group had moved sixteen kilometres away into the Gorely swamp.)

'How many men in the group?'

'Thirty.'

'You're lying! We know there are more than that.'

Rybak smiled in a superior kind of way. He felt a need to demonstrate some slight degree of scorn for the interrogator's lack of information.

'There were more. But now there are thirty. You know, fighting, people get killed.'

The interrogator stretched himself contentedly in his chair.

'So, our lads have been getting at you, have they? Good, good. They'll soon have your skins, all of you.'

Rybak didn't reply. The interrogator's mood was clearly improving. It looked as if they had got very little from Sotnikov, which left him room to make his answers up—it'd be up to them to try and check them. And it also looked as if the interrogator's attitude towards Rybak was beginning to mellow and Rybak felt that he should try to encourage that shift, so that he could make use

115

of it later.

'Right!' The interrogator leant back in his chair. 'Now tell me which of you two was shooting last night? Our people saw one of you run away and the other start firing. Was that you?'

'No, it wasn't me,' said Rybak, but not too firmly. He found it very uncomfortable to have to defend himself by laying the blame on Sotnikov. But what else could he do—take it on himself?

'Then it was the other one? Right?'

He left that question unanswered. Rybak merely thought, I wish you were dead, you bastard! That was a clever trap! What possible answer was there?

But Portnov didn't press the point.

'Right, that's clear. What's his name?'

'Whose?'

'Your companion.'

His name! Why did he suddenly need to know his name? But if Sotnikov hadn't given it, then it certainly wasn't up to Rybak to do so. It looked as if a lie was needed, but Rybak wasn't sure how best to do it.

'I don't know,' he said in the end. 'I've not been in the group for long.'

'You don't know?', Portnov repeated the question reproach-fully. 'And you say the headman's name is Sych? Is that the name you have for him in the group?'

Rybak searched his memory—he didn't remember even having heard the headman's name or a nickname.

'I don't know. In the village I heard people calling him Pyotr.'

'Ah, Pyotr.'

It seemed to Rybak that Portnov was getting mixed up, but then it occurred to him that the interrogator was trying to confuse him.

'Right. So where were you born? Mogilev?'

'Near Gomel,' Rybak repeated patiently, 'In the Rechitskiy region.'

'Name?'

'Whose?'

'Yours.'

'Rybak.'

'Where's the rest of your group?'

'In the . . . in the Borkovskiy forest.'

'How far?'

116

'Where from?'

'From here?'

'I don't know precisely. It'd be about eighteen kilometres.'

'Villages? Degtyarnya, Ulyanovka. And there's that one . . . Draguny.'

Portnov glanced at a paper lying on the table in front of him.

'And what connections does your group have with this woman Avginya Okun?'

'Demchikha? None at all. We just went into the house to hide and get something to eat. And then there were the children there . . .'

'Oh, the children were a surprise to you, were they? Good for them! No connection, you say?'

'That's right, none, Avginya's nothing to do with any of this.'

The interrogator rose briskly from the chair, and hitched up his trousers which were slipping from his belt.

'She's innocent, is she? Yet she took you in? Hid you in the loft? Do you think she didn't know who she was hiding? She knew perfectly well! In other words she was aiding and abetting. And do you know what the penalties are for that under wartime laws?'

Rybak knew all too well what the penalties were for that under wartime laws. He realised that perhaps the time had come to abandon the impossible task of protecting Demchikha. It was plain that the interrogator would react to every such attempt like a bull to a red flag, and he decided to try not to antagonise him. It was up to Demchikha now to get herself out of it if she could.

'All right then!' The interrogator walked over to the window, and turned sharply on his heel. His hands were thrust deep into his trouser pockets and his jacket was wide open over his chest. 'We'll talk again. But I must admit that you're a lad with a good head on his shoulders. Maybe we'll let you live. You don't believe me?' The interrogator grinned ironically. 'We can. Your Soviets never could. But we can punish and we can show mercy. Depending on who it is. Got it?'

He came and stood very close to Rybak, who, feeling that this was probably the end of the interrogation, respectfully got up from the chair. The interrogator only came up to his shoulder, and Rybak had the sudden thought that he could easily strangle the little man. But the stupidity of the idea almost frightened him, and he looked with feigned gratitude into the alert, authoritatively cold eyes of the interrogator.

117

'So! You'll tell us everything. And we'll check it all—get that right for a start. If you're not lying, you can stay alive, join the *politsai*, and serve Great Germany . . .'

'What, me?' Rybak could hardly believe his ears.

He felt as if the floor was swaying beneath his feet and the walls of this filthy room were falling away. His total confusion gave way to a distinct feeling of freedom, of space, and he even imagined he could feel the fresh breath of wind.

'Yes, you. Do you accept? You needn't answer straight away. Go on, think about it. But remember—the truth, or that's your lot. Gamanyuk!'

Before Rybak, totally shattered, could think what would happen next, the door opened and Stas appeared.

'Back to the cellar!'

Stas looked in bewilderment at the interrogator.

'But . . . Budila's waiting . . .'

'Back to the cellar!' bellowed the interrogator. 'Are you deaf, or what?'

Stas pulled himself together.

'*Jawohl*, to the cellar. This way, *bitte*!'

Rybak left the room, as he had entered, totally confused, although this time for an entirely different reason. Although he was not yet completely aware of the full complexity of what he had just been through, and even less of what the future held, he already felt sharply and joyfully that he was going to live! The possibility of life had reappeared, and that was the main thing. Everything else he could think about later.

'So it's been postponed?' Stas grabbed him by the arm of his sheepskin as they emerged into the yard.

'Yes, it's been postponed,' said Rybak firmly, and looked challengingly for the first time at the red, scornfully smiling face of the *politsai*. Stas let out a hoarse chuckle, like a goat bleating.

'You'll not get away with it! You'll talk! Voluntarily, because you have to—we'll have your guts!'

He's either stupid or he's kidding, thought Rybak. But now he wasn't much worried about Stas. He had acquired a defender.

13

It was his weakness that saved Sotnikov. As soon as Budila started the torture, he passed out. They brought him round by throwing a bucket of water over him, but his recovery didn't last long. His mind went blank again, and his body didn't react to the thumbscrews or the special steel pincers which Budila used to pull out his fingernails. After they'd wasted half an hour or so, two *politsai* dragged Sotnikov out of the room and threw him into the cell along with the headman.

For some time he lay silent on the straw in his soaked clothes, his hands covered in blood, groaning quietly. Sometimes he was conscious for a few moments, but kept on lapsing back into unconsciousness. When the footsteps of the *politsai* had faded away outside the door, the headman Pyotr crawled over to him on hands and knees.

'Ay-yai! I didn't recognise you. Look what they've done to you . . .'

Sotnikov heard a new voice close to him, and it seemed familiar, but his confused mind was in no state to establish who this man was. But the man seemed to be well disposed to him, or so Sotnikov judged from his voice, so he asked him for help.

'Water!'

He heard the man get up and start hammering, insistently, although not very loudly, on the door of the cell.

'Hell! No one's listening.'

Although his thoughts were still not clear, Sotnikov realised that there was no help to be had here. So he asked for nothing more, just tried to forget where he was and what had happened, and stayed alone with his torment. But he desperately wanted a drink. A sort of burning hot mist wreathed around him. In imagination Sotnikov stumbled along on feet that felt as if they were made of cotton wool until by a fence he saw a well with a bucket dangling on a chain. With cotton wool hands he began to lower the bucket into the well, when suddenly from the blackness of the bottomless shaft a brood of cats hurled themselves into his face. Sotnikov had always detested cats, and almost in terror he flung himself away from the well handle, and gradually began to come to his senses. But then he was on a street in his own town before the war. Suddenly he saw Redkin, his orderly who had served him for a long time, coming towards him with a handful of damp military water flasks, all full of water. Sotnikov seized one of them, but as he did so it turned into a gas mask, with no water to be seen anywhere . . .

After some time he imagined that he got hold of a mess tin of water, and drank long and deep. But the water was warm and brackish, and didn't quench his thirst, just swelled out his stomach uncomfortably. This longed-for drink brought him no relief, but rather increased his suffering, and he began to feel sick. The midday sun had made the dug-out where he stood very hot, and there was nothing around him but burning sand and clumps of prickly dried grass. He was still drinking when quite close to him he heard a loud shouted order from Colonel Loginov, the commander of the battery: 'Keep in time, keep in time!' Sotnikov was both surprised and alarmed—it seemed strange that he should have taken time out from the bombardment to have a drink of water. He was afraid that he might not be able to keep up the tempo of the sequence of firing orders, which instead of the prescribed six to ten seconds seemed to be taking more than a minute.

Then these hallucinations faded, and his mind began a meaningless rambling punctuated by strange fleeting images. The only thing that remained constant and real was the pain.

When they brought Rybak back to the cell, Sotnikov was lying like a corpse in the straw, covered from head to foot in his greatcoat. Rybak knelt beside him, turned back the greatcoat and took his hand. Sotnikov's torn fingers were stuck together in bloody clusters, and Rybak was horrified by the thought that they might have done the same thing to him. This first time violence had passed him by, but what would tomorrow bring?

'Jailer—this man . . . he needs water,' said Pyotr from his corner, while Stas was locking the door.

'You don't call me jailer, you call me Mr. *Politsai*!' barked Stas maliciously.

All right then, *politsai.* I'm sorry. This man is dying.'

'So should all bandits. You as well.'

The door crashed shut, and it was dark again. Pyotr sighed and dropped back on to the straw in the corner.

'They're wild animals.'

'Be quiet,' said Rybak. 'They'll hear you.'

'Let them hear. What is there left to be afraid of?'

The outer door closed too, the *politsai*'s footsteps died away on the stairs. It was very quiet, and in the silence they could just make out someone in another cell sobbing quietly, spasmodically in gulps. It must be a child or perhaps a woman. Sotnikov, still unconscious on the straw, was muttering something.

'They've maimed him for life,' said Pyotr. 'Will he live?'

Rybak thought, he'll not live for long. And then he had a sudden and penetrating and hopeful thought—if Sotnikov were to die, then his, Rybak's, chances of living would be that much beter. There were no other witnesses.

He realised, of course, all the inhumanity this idea contained, but no matter how much he thought about it, he kept on returning to the one idea—that it would be better like that. Not only for him, Rybak, but also for Sotnikov, who after everything that had happened to him might just as well be dead already. Rybak on the other hand had a chance of getting out of it, and then he would take care of these bastards and make them pay for Sotnikov's death and his sufferings. He hadn't the least intention of revealing the partisans' secrets, or of joining the *politsai*, although he realised that it might be difficult to avoid that. But the important thing was to gain time—everything depended on how long he could make them delay things.

Sotnikov was breathing heavily and huskily, groaning slightly. Rybak thought, no, he'll never hold out. Even a fit man wouldn't last long in this place, so Sotnikov hadn't much chance.

'I see that you've come out of it better than him,' said the old man deliberately and it seemed to Rybak meaningfully. His words irritated Rybak—what business was it of his anyway?

'Obviously it's still to come—they won't let you get away as easily as that.'

Rybak looked angrily into the corner—these unsought prophecies of the old man were driving him mad. Why should he know whether he'd get away with it or not? His balance sheet was different from everyone else's. He almost believed that he had a special providence watching over him, and he tried to think everything through to the last detail.

But this place was obviously not very suitable for cogitation. He had only just begun to concentrate on his own worries when steps came down the staircase again. He thought that another prisoner was being brought in, but the footsteps stopped outside their cell, the bolt was flung back, and there stood Stas once more.

'Here's some water. Quick, take it! And make sure this bandit's back on his feet tomorrow! As for you, you old devil, off you come to Budila!'

Rybak suppressed the fear which had leapt into his throat, and took the tin of cold water from Stas. Pyotr looked uncertainly at Stas from his corner.

'Do you know why?'

The *politsai* bellowed with genuine mirth.

'I know all right. He wants to play ball with you. Get moving!'

The old man dragged himself wearily to his feet, picked his coat from the floor and, with his head bent, left the cell. The heavy door slammed to again.

Rybak knelt by Sotnikov and began to try to bring him round. But Sotnikov merely groaned. Then with one hand Rybak tipped the water tin and with the other raised Sotnikov's head and managed to get a little water between his lips. Sotnikov shuddered, but then thirstily set his lips to the jagged rim of the tin, and swallowed a few mouthfuls greedily but with difficulty.

'Who is it?'

'Me. How are you? Any better?'

'Rybak? You! Give me some more!'

Rybak held his head again, his teeth banging against the tin. Sotnikov drank and then fell back limp to the floor.

'They gave you a bad time of it,' said Rybak.

'It was bad enough, certainly,' sighed Sotnikov.

Rybak solicitously arranged the greatcoat over him, and sat back against the wall and listened absent-mindedly to his companion's noisy breathing, which gradually became more regular.

'How do you feel now?'

'All right now. Better. What about you?'

'What?'

'Did they beat you up?'

122

This question took Rybak by surprise. He couldn't think how to explain briefly to Sotnikov why he hadn't been tortured.

'No, not much.'

Sotnikov closed his eyes. His exhausted, grey, stubble-covered face could hardly be seen in the half darkness against the grey straw. His chest was still wheezing. Then it came into Rybak's mind that now while they had the chance they ought to agree something of what they would say on further questioning.

'Listen, I think I can trick them,' he whispered, leaning close to Sotnikov's ear. Sotnikov opened his eyes in amazement—the whites reflecting dimly the light from the ceiling. 'But we must stick to the same story. First, we were going to get food. The farm was burnt down so we went to Lyesiny, and then . . .'

'I shan't tell them anything,' Sotnikov broke in.

Rybak listened to see if he could hear anyone nearby, but everything seemed quiet. There was just a sound of voices and footsteps from upstairs, directly over the cell. But no one would be able to hear from upstairs.

'Drop that, don't be stupid. We've got to tell them something. So listen. We're from Dubovoi's group, and he's in the Borkovskiy forest. Let them check that.'

Sotnikov caught his breath.

'But Dubovoi really *is* there.'

'So what?'

Rybak was beginning to feel angry—the last thing he needed was a man who wouldn't agree with his plan. Of course Dubovoi and his group were in the Borkovskiy forest, but the fact of telling the Germans where they were wouldn't make things any the worse for them—the *politsai* wouldn't be able to get near them anyway. The remains of their own group were in a far worse position.

'Listen. Just you listen to me! If we don't string them along a bit, don't trick them, in a day or two we'll be finished. Got it? We have to play just a little at traitors. We can't do more than we've got strength for!'

He could hear Sotnikov tensing, getting on his guard. He grew quieter, and his breathing faded away—as if he were thinking hard about something.

'Nothing will come of it,' he said in the end.

'What do you mean, nothing'll come of it? And if we do nothing, then what? Death's the easiest thing in the world to find.'

What a fool the man is, thought Rybak. He hadn't expected such unreasonable obstinacy. Of course, he had one foot in the grave already, so it didn't matter much to him. He doesn't even want the trouble of exerting his mind to avoid dragging a comrade in there after him.

'You listen,' Rybak whispered hotly, after a pause. 'We've got to play them like a pike that's taken the bait. Otherwise when we reel in, the line'll break, and that's our lot. We've got to pretend to go along with them. You know that they've proposed that I should join the *politsai*!' Rybak said, although he wasn't sure that he wanted to say it.

Sotnikov's eyebrows fluttered open, and his eyes glinted with a muted and disturbed concern.

'Did they now? And what are you going to do—make a break for it?'

'Don't worry, I'm not going to try to escape. I'm going to make a deal with them.'

'Make a deal with them?' Sotnikov hissed, poison in his voice.

'All right then, we just get shot otherwise,' Rybak finally broke, and almost screamed at Sotnikov. He cut his shout short and cursed himself. The hell with it! If Sotnikov didn't want to go along with the idea, that's his look out. Rybak would fight for himself to the last.

Sotnikov was breathing less easily, although it wasn't clear whether it was from emotion or from the phlegm he was trying to cough up. His chest whistled and wheezed like a kettle on the hob, and Rybak thought anxiously, is he dying? But he didn't die, and soon, when he had controlled his breathing, he said:

'You're wasting your time crawling to the bastards! You're dishonouring the army. They'll never let us out of here alive.'

'That's what you say. If we were to try . . .'

'Try for whom?' Sotnikov burst out, angrily, and sighed. For a moment he coughed in torment, then breathed heavily, and whispered in a failing voice, 'You don't get brought in by the *politsai* for a game of cards.'

Certainly not, Rybak agreed silently. But he was going into this game to try to win his life—wasn't that stake enough for the most desperate game? And the result would be clear, provided that they didn't kill him or torture him in interrogation. If he could only get out of the cage, he wouldn't do anything bad. He was no enemy of

124

his own people.

'Don't worry,' he said. 'I'm not sewn together with thin thread. I won't come apart.'

Sotnikov laughed an unnaturally short laugh.

'You're a fool. Who did you think you'd be tangling with?'

'You'll see.'

'It's a machine. Either you'll serve it, or it'll grind you to powder!'

'Me—serve them?'

'Just wait until you begin.'

No, thought Rybak, there's no chance of getting that madman to agree. Just as in life so at death's door that thick-headed stubbornness is above everything, those principles. The whole thing's a matter of character, at least that's the way Rybak saw it. But surely everyone realises that in the game called life, the man who cheats best comes out with most. And how could it be otherwise? Of course fascism is a machine, a machine grinding half the world beneath its wheels, how can you try to beat it with your bare hands in open combat? It could be that it'd be better and more effective to try to shove a spoke in its wheels from the side. Better to catch on and be towed along behind, to give yourself a chance of slipping away on the sly to your own people.

Sotnikov was quiet, or perhaps he had lapsed into semi-consciousness, and Rybak stopped trying to talk him round. Let him act as he thought fit—he, Rybak, would act according to his own opinions.

He lay down on his side, drew his legs up, and pulled the collar of his sheepskin higher. Until things really got moving, it would be no bad thing to snatch an hour's sleep so that his head would be clearer, because it wouldn't be long, for sure, before the real testing-time began. But he believed in his lucky star, and gradually he was managing to convince himself that his relations with the *politsai* were moving in the right direction. If only Sotnikov's absurd obstinacy didn't ruin his plans. But it looked as if Sotnikov wouldn't last much longer. It was odd and unpleasant to think of, hope for the early death of a comrade, but that was the best solution. Sotnikov's death seemed to him to be the only way out of this situation for himself.

Sunk in thought, Rybak didn't at first notice something living quietly scamper over his boot, and then again. He moved his leg.

Then suddenly and clearly he saw the rat, its grey body flickered to the wall and froze; its long thin tail lay on the straw. Rybak shivered, then lashed out with his foot. The rat, squeaking on a high note, scuttered away to hide in the dark corner. But Rybak realised from the squeaking and rustling in the straw that the rat he had seen was not the only one. The best thing would be to throw something at them, but nothing came to hand. Rybak tore his hat from his head and slung it into the corner.

When the squeaking died away, he crawled over on all fours, collected his hat, and propped himself up once more against the wall. But he couldn't sleep. While he waited for the rats to launch another attack, he covered Sotnikov's bare foot with his coat, then sat peering into the corner, vaguely disgusted and afraid.

14

It was a long time before they brought Pyotr back, nearly at sunset, when it was already quite dark in the cell and the window high in the wall hardly showed any of the meagre twilight of the frosty day outside. Even when the door opened there was none of the former bright light. His white head sunk on his chest, the headman silently stepped into the cell and sank down in his dark, rat-infested corner.

By the wall Rybak tried not to move. He shrank back as far as he could into the darkness of the stinking cell. He was afraid that they might summon him out again, although he realised that this did not depend on the guards. But they took no one, the door closed again, and there was the sound of the bolt being thrust safely home. But the *politsai*—not Stas this time, but another one—didn't return up the steps. His footsteps moved off in a different direction along the corridor. Soon, somewhere in the depths of the cellar, there was a sound of more bolts, a muffled order, and the sound of a woman's brief sobs.

This time it was women they were taking for interrogation.

As soon as all was quiet in the cellar again, Rybak gradually began to recover his self-control. For the time being the worst of the trouble had passed him by and taken another, which was reassuring in a way. It was as if he had been given another chance of survival. Although of course, what chance he had was worse than doubtful.

Rybak didn't have the slightest desire to start a conversation with the headman, who, it seemed, had not been tortured, or at least nothing like as badly as Sotnikov. But the fact that he had settled down in his corner without saying a word unsettled Rybak.

'Well? Got out of it?' Rybak asked, deliberately cheerful.

After a short pause Pyotr replied in a gloomy voice, 'No, we won't get out of it. We're in a bad way.'

'Never worse,' Rybak agreed.

The headman blew his nose, smoothed his moustache with an accustomed gesture, and said, almost casually, as if not addressing anyone in particular: 'They tried to persuade me to inform on you. About your group, and so on.'

'Well!' Rybak was surprised, and wrinkled his forehead, thinking of his recent conversation with Sotnikov. 'You mean, to spy on us?'

'That's it. I've lived sixty-seven years, and in my old age to be asked to do a thing like that. No, that's not my sort of line at all . . .'

Next to him, Sotnikov moved in the straw, and raised himself on his elbows seemingly frightened.

'Who's that?'

'It's the headman from Lyesiny,' said Rybak gloomily.

Sotnikov fell silent and lay down on the straw again, trying to sort out the confusion between reality and the half-waking dreams that ran through his mind. He felt very ill. His leg hurt as before from the bullet in the thigh, his fingers were in flames, and his chest heaved and felt close to bursting. Most of the time his mind was wallowing in a black and bottomless pit, and when it briefly surfaced he could not immediately come to terms with what was going on around him. But this time he remembered their nocturnal visit to Lyesiny, the headman Pyotr, and now that he was aware of him beside him, he understood everything at once. True, Sotnikov had no particular sympathy for Pyotr; the headman was not Demchikha. Still it was unpleasant to have to admit that this old man had been dragged by them into this place, from which, probably, there was no way out.

The conversation broke off at this point. Rybak and Pyotr sat quietly in their corners. Now that the light outside had vanished, the window scarcely showed against the ceiling, although they could still see the bars that divided it into four. The cell itself was almost completely dark. No one wanted to talk, and each let himself sink into his unpleasant reflections.

Then there were footsteps again on the stairs. They heard the outer door open; then the bolt on their door slid back with an unexpected clang. They all tensed, all alarmed by the only question in such situations—whom had they come for? But apparently this time they were not taking anyone away. On the contrary—someone else was being brought into the cell.

'Get moving!'

Someone completely invisible in the darkness slipped almost

inaudibly through the door and stood silent and motionless near Rybak's feet. When the door slammed to and the *politsai* had bolted up and gone away whistling, Rybak spoke into the darkness.

'Who's there?'

'Me.'

It was immediately clear that it was a child. The small figure of the new prisoner shrank back against the door, and said nothing more.

'Who's me? What's your name?'

'Basya.'

Basya? Basya? Sounds like a Jewish name, but how's she turned up here, wondered Rybak. All the Jews from the town had been liquidated the previous autumn, and everyone had thought that no one had escaped, so where had this one come from? And why had they put her in with them and not with Demchikha?

'Where are you from?' Rybak asked.

The girl didn't reply. He tried another question.

'How old are you?'

'Thirteen.'

Pyotr moved in his corner.

'Surely you can't be the daughter of Meer the shoemaker?'

'Yes,' the girl agreed quietly.

'But Meer was killed along with all the rest? How did you manage to escape? You must have hidden.'

Again there was no reply. Indeed Rybak was not waiting for an answer. He had suddenly lost all interest in the child. He was far too concerned about something else; why had she been brought in here? There must be somewhere else left in the cellar, there were women in a cell close by. Why had they put the girl in with the men? What did it mean?

'And what do they want from you?' Pyotr went on questioning Basya as if there were nothing untoward in her presence.

'To tell them who hid me.'

'So that's what they're after. And you haven't told them?'

Basya was as quiet as if she weren't even breathing. She didn't reply.

'And you mustn't tell them,' the headman said approvingly. 'You mustn't tell them about that. People did you a good turn, so keep quiet about it, even if they beat you. Or have they been beating you already?'

This time instead of a reply a sob suddenly came from the corner, followed by suppressed, painful weeping. It didn't last long, but it contained so much of genuine childish despair that everyone in the cell was touched by it. They could hear Sotnikov lying on the straw carefully holding his breath.

'Rybak.'

'I'm here.'

'There was some water left.'

'You want a drink?'

'Give her some water! Don't just sit there!'

Rybak felt along the wall for the tin and offered it to the girl.

'Don't cry. Here, have a drink.'

Basya drank a little, calmed down and sat by the door.

'Come over here,' called Pyotr. 'There's room here. We'll sit together. Here, feel your way along the wall.'

Basya obediently got up and moved silently on her bare feet in the darkness over to the old man. He moved over to make room for her beside him.

'Yes. We've all been caught. What else can they do to us?'

Rybak didn't respond. He had no wish to keep up a conversation. Beside him Sotnikov was groaning quietly. They waited. Their entire attention was turned towards the stairs—that's where trouble came from.

They didn't have long to wait.

After about a quarter of an hour they heard a voice in the yard yelling angrily:

'Get on, you cow!' and no less an angry reply, 'Go and burn in hell you bastard.'—'Get moving, or I'll damned well move you!' a man's voice yelled back. There were footsteps and curses on the stairs. There was no doubt about it—they were bringing Demchikha down.

But for some reason they didn't put her back in her old cell. The *politsai* stopped outside their door, the bolt rattled back, and old familiar Stas flung Demchikha through the door. The woman stumbled, fell over Rybak's feet, and began to scream in the darkness.

'Who d'you think you're shoving, you bastard? There are men in here, my God.'

'Get in there. The devil won't eat you,' bellowed Stas. 'You'll last till morning.'

130

'And what happens in the morning?' Rybak suddenly asked.

'In the morning, *gross alles kaput! Versteh?*'

'*Kaput?* What does he mean, *kaput?*' ran round Rybak's fearful and confused mind. But the awful meaning of that short word was far too clear for there to be any prolonged doubt as to its meaning. And that clarity struck the mind like a hammer blow.

So the morning would be the end!

Almost unaware of what he was doing, Rybak mechanically folded his legs under him to make room for the woman to sit by the door. She was still sobbing and snuffling, and then she began to calm down. For a moment they were all silent, and then Pyotr said reasonably from his corner:

'Well, what can you do if you've been caught? We just have to be patient. Whereabouts are you from, woman?'

'Me? I'm from Poddubya, if you know it.'

'I know it, of course I know it. And who are you?'

'I'm Demka Okun's wife.'

In an attempt to get away from his gloomy thoughts about the morning, Rybak began to listen to Demchikha. He didn't want to join the conversation and reveal who he was, the more so as Demchikha had probably not recognised him in the darkness. They had already seen enough of her tempestuous character, and now that they were in this situation, Rybak thought that the woman might easily start a fearful and distressing row—she had cause enough. But she gradually cooled down, and blew her nose again. Her voice became more controlled, normal, the same voice with which she had spoken to them in the village.

'Ye-es,' Pyotr sounded concerned. 'And Demka's in the army . . .'

'Yes, Demka's out there having a miserable time of it, and I'm at home and everyone mocks me. They've taken everything! Who's looking after the children? How will they manage without me? Oh, my own litle children . . .'

She broke off and started weeping again, and this time no one tried to console her or calm her down—no one felt capable of it. The cell still echoed to Stas's ominous words, they oppressed everyone, frightened them, and drove them all to despair—all with the exception of the headman who remained as calm and reasonable as ever. Suddenly Demchikha sighed, as if she had cried herself out, and said in a calmer voice:

'What people they are. Like wild beasts! Just look what a devil Pavka's turned into.'

'Portnov, you mean?' Pyotr took up the conversation.

'Yes. I remember him as a young man—they used to call him Pavka then. He studied to be a teacher. Evon's mother lived at the farm, and in the summer he'd go along for milk or apples. She could never see enough of him. He was such a pleasant kindly lad. Always said "Good day" to people, and shook hands with all the peasants.'

'I know Portnov,' said Pyotr. 'He used to go round the villages lecturing against God. Spoke very well . . .'

'He was a rotten pig. And he still is. The only thing is not everyone knows it. That's what you call your cultured man!'

'That young *politsai*'s over from your way, too, isn't he?'

'That Stas? He's from our village! Filipov's youngest. He cut someone's throat and went to jail, and he went over to them right from the start. And look what he's turned into—it's terrible! In the village it was always the Jews he used to be getting at. They say he killed quite a few of them. Building up a good name for himself with the Germans—God save us all. Filled an entire hut with bodies. Now he's got on to us Christians.'

'That's the way it is,' agreed Pyotr. 'Starting with the Jews, and now look, ending up with us.'

'They should all be strung up on an aspen tree, those bastards.'

'I always think'—the headman diverted the conversation anxiously—'I can understand the Germans. We know they're fascists, foreigners, you can expect anything from them. But our own people, people who were born and brought up here! How can you understand them? You get a man who's lived here all his life, eaten our bread, looked people in the eye—and then he gets hold of a rifle and goes round trying to shoot people! And actually *does* shoot them! God knows how many people they've killed already . . .'

'What about the other one . . . what's his name . . . Budila?' Rybak butted in, unable to restrain himself any longer.

'There are plenty like him. Budila and quite a few others. Some from round here and some from God knows where. Just people who used to like robbing and raping and murdering. Now they've got freedom to do just as they like.' The headman of Lyesiny put his views gravely, in his deep bass voice. Then Demchikha, as if she had suddenly remembered something, broke in impatiently.

'They were saying that Khodoronok, the one who got shot last night, has died. So perish them all, the bunch of filth!'

'They won't all die,' sighed Pyotr, 'Not unless our people kill them.'

Sotnikov moved in the straw, took a deep breath, and tried to sit up.

'Have you thought that way for long?' he muttered hoarsely.

'What do you think, lad? It's clear to everybody.'

'You say it's clear? How did you get to be a headman, then?'

There was an awkward silence. No one spoke, all put on their guard by this far-reaching question. Finally Pyotr seemed to get control of himself and spoke in a voice which seemed suddenly to tremble.

'I became a headman! If only you knew . . . It's not easy to tell you. Although time's running out—it's too late to keep it a secret any more. I resisted it as much as I could. I didn't go to the regional capital. It's not as if I'm a fool, not as if I didn't understand what it was all about. Then one night there was a knock on my window. I opened it, and there outside is the man who used to be regional party secretary, the head of the proper Soviet militia, and two others, all armed. The secretary knew me. I'd taken him home after a meeting during the collectivisation period. Well, word for word, he said to me, "We've heard that your name's been put forward for headman. Well, take it. If not, they'll appoint Budila, and that'll mean misery for everyone." So I agreed. Took it on my own head.'

'Yes,' Rybak said uncertainly.

'For six months I was between the devil and the deep blue sea. Until I broke away. Now what is there left to do? Just die, that's all.'

'Dying's an easy thing,' growled Rybak, trying to end a conversation which he found very unpleasant. Not that what the headman had said had come as a complete surprise to him; Rybak had begun to guess something of the kind after his own inter-rogation by Portnov. But now he was completely engrossed in his own worries, and chiefly concerned lest some of the views he had expressed in the cell might reach the ears of the *politsai* and break his last thread of hope.

Sotnikov lay silently on the straw, his eyes open. It sounded as if the headman was speaking the truth. But what had happened, then? Sotnikov was overtaken by a strong feeling that they had been stupidly mistaken as far as Pyotr was concerned. But whose fault was it? No one could have foreseen the way things would turn out—a chain of appalling coincidences had led to this conclusion. Although there again they had to dig deeper into the story. But in the case of Demchikha everything was absolutely clear. Demchikha stood before them as a living reproach to their unforgivable lack of concern. As he listened apprehensively to the woman's voice, Sotnikov waited for her to begin cursing them with her dying words. He couldn't think what he could say in reply. But time passed, and she went on venting all her rage and despair on the Germans and the *politsai*—she didn't even refer to him and Rybak, as though they had absolutely nothing to do with the catastrophe that had overtaken her. Nor had she reacted to Stas's ominous announcement. Maybe she had not understood what he meant, or maybe she had simply not been paying any attention to what he said.

Even Sotnikov, who was ready to die, found that announcement frightening. He couldn't be absolutely certain what it meant; either the *politsai* had merely been trying to scare them, or they really had decided to get rid of the lot of them at one stroke. But surely two deaths would have been enough for them—his and Rybak's. What sense was there in slaughtering the unfortunate Demchikha, the ill-starred headman, and the child? It seemed unlikely, but, thought Sotnikov, that was what was going to happen. A scorpion must sting, or what kind of scorpion does he show himself to be? That seemed to be the reason why they had all been put into the one cell—the death cell.

15

Almost unaware of it, Rybak dozed off where he sat, hunched against the wall. But it could hardly be called sleep—more an exhausted semi-consciousness that lasted about an hour. But soon fear woke him, and Rybak opened his eyes, at first not fully aware of where he was. Beside him in the darkness people were talking quietly, one of them in a familiar child's voice, which immediately reminded him of Basya's presence. Sometimes the child was interrupted by a husky old man's whisper—that would be Pyotr putting in his weighty words. Rybak listened to`their quiet night-time talk which reminded him of the rustling of thatch in the wind.

'At first I wanted to run after them when they were being taken away. I jumped over the fence, but then Auntie Praskovya waved at me and said, "Don't go, don't go whatever you do. Hide!" So I ran back behind the vegetable garden, and crawled into a bunch of osiers. Perhaps you know them, there's a big clump behind the gardens down by the stream? It's very thick. It's only a couple of yards away from the path to the graveyard, but if you sit quiet and don't move, no one could ever find you. So I got in there, made a hole for myself among the dry leaves, and waited. I waited and waited and no one called. It was getting dark and I was frightened. Then I thought I heard something moving, creeping round, and then stopping to listen. I thought it was a wolf. I was so afraid of wolves! And I didn't go to sleep at all. I just dozed off a little when it was beginning to get light. When I woke I was very hungry. But I was afraid to come out of the trees. I could hear a lot of noise from the street, and carts. They were taking everything out of the houses and moving it all away. I just stayed where I was for another day and night. I don't remember how much longer. When the women went down the path to do their washing in the river, I could see their legs through the leaves. They all went past. And I was so hungry I didn't have the strength to crawl out. I just sat and cried to myself. But then once someone stopped near the trees. I froze, just lay there holding my breath. And then I heard someone saying quietly, "Basya, Basya, where are you?" I looked out and there was Auntie Praskovya bending down looking for me.'

'Don't you tell us who it was. There's no need for us to know,' Pyotr interrupted calmly.

'Well, this lady gave me a bundle with some bread and dripping. I took it and ate it all at once. There was only a tiny bit of bread left. And then my stomach began to hurt. It hurt so much I wanted to die. I prayed to Mummy and to God, prayed for death.'

By the wall Rybak huddled tighter, shivering—all this sounded so familiar, as if he was hearing the story of an old woman, and not a thirteen-year-old girl. Her story had immediately called to his mind a recollection of a ninety-year-old woman from a village in the forest on this side of the railway. They had come out of the forest to ask where the Germans were and to rest for an hour or so in the warmth and, of course, to get a bite to eat if they could. In the cottage which stood alone there was no one left but a god-forsaken deaf old woman who was sitting on the stove, her bare feet dangling on the floor. While they sat and smoked she wearily reproached the Lord God for refusing to let her die and for making her go on living her useless old woman's life. Alone and without any family, even at the end of the last war, she had had to live among people she hardly knew, strangers, and she had had to bring up their children and look after the house. Clearly the people she lived with reckoned that the old woman would last another five years or so, by which time the children would be grown up enough, and her time would come and she'd be off to the graveyard. But her time didn't come, not in five, nor yet fifteen years, and the old woman stayed alive among these strangers. During this time the babies grew up, the man of the house was killed in the Finnish war, and the woman could hardly make ends meet—what use was a helpless old woman to her? But death still didn't come. When Rybak and the others left her, they all wished her from the heart a speedy end to her stay in this world, and she thanked them sincerely, and went on praying for the same thing. Now here again he was hearing the same prayer—but this time from a child. What had the world come to?

'Then I began to feel better. Once I was very frightened in the morning. I had just dropped off, when I heard an animal creeping along the bank under the bushes. And it was a cat. A great big grey cat, probably from the village, that had been left on its own, and was looking for food. Catching fish. You know, it'd stand on the bank, very still, step into the water, and then it'd jump! It got out of the water soaking wet with a fish in its mouth. I though if only I could catch fish like that. I tried to take the fish from the cat, but I couldn't. The cat went off and ate it all under another bush. It didn't leave a scrap. But later on I made friends with it. Sometimes it used to come during the day, creep in beside me and lie there and miaow. I used to stroke it and fall asleep. And it was very clever! If any one came anywhere near, its fur would bristle, and I'd know that I had to take care. When I was very hungry, I'd go into the vegetable garden at night. There were still some cucumbers in Hunchback Zalman's patch, that'd gone to seed, and some carrots. But the cat wouldn't eat the carrots, and I felt sorry for it . . .'

'It should have caught some mice,' said Demchikha in the darkness. 'There were some people in Poddubya near us who had a cat that used to bring rabbits home. It's as true as I'm sitting here. Once it brought home such a huge rabbit that it couldn't even drag it into the loft—wasn't strong enough. Yefim went out one morning and found this rabbit by the corner of the house.'

'She probably had kittens.' Pyotr suggested.

'That's right, she did.'

'Well, that's obvious then, she was doing it for her kittens. Just like any mother. Then what happened, Basya?'

'I stayed where I was,' whispered Basya, quietly and trustingly. 'Auntie . . . well, the woman . . . used to bring me bread sometimes. Then it got very cold, and it rained, and the leaves began to fall. Once someone saw me in the morning—a man. He didn't say anything, just walked past. But I was so afraid that I trembled until dark. That night when it was pouring with rain I came out and I wandered all over the place until I found a barn. I stayed there for three days. It was good there, dry, but then they came to search the place. They were looking for some rye, but they nearly found me. So I went into the byre—there were pigs there. And I lived with them. At night I got in between the sow and the piglets and slept. The sow was quiet but the boar used to bite me, curse him . . .'

'Oh, my God, the things she's suffered, poor child!' sighed Demchikha.

'No. It was nice and warm there.'

'What did you do for food? Did people bring it to you?'

'No one knew I was there. Food—well, I used to get something out of the trough.'

'Oh, the state that people have been brought to, Oh God, Oh God. So who caught you then in the end?'

'The *politsai*. I overslept one day—the snow had started. I jumped up to run across the street—there was an empty house there where I used to hide. I was just crossing and there they were. They shouted, and I hid behind the maple trees—there's a very big maple just there . . .'

'You mean just opposite the chemist's,' said Demchikha—'Where Ignalii Supron used to live . . .'

'What does that matter to you?' Pyotr broke in sharply. 'It doesn't matter who lived there. Why ask?'

Demchikha sounded offended.

'I only asked. And if she said who, what does it matter?'

'Never mind! What happened then? You tell us your story, it'll make the night go quicker.'

Shut up, you old fool, thought Rybak crossly. It's odd how anxiously he seems to be waiting for the morning. Or perhaps he's hoping to be set free tomorrow?

He wanted to interrupt Basya. What was the point of telling all this story here? Everyone knew that walls sometimes had ears. But then he thought the hell with the lot of them. They were no concern of his. And anyway it was probably far too late to try to hid anything or protect anyone. If Stas had been speaking the truth, then they would all die in the morning.

'Well, they started shouting, and I ran away. I ran and I ran over the snow until I got behind the vegetable gardens again. It wasn't far to the forest. But they caught up with me, grabbed my arms and brought me here. And then they beat me a lot . . . and then . . .'

A frightened yell from Basya brought Pyotr from his place in the corner, and Rybak realised what the matter was—rats. They had got so brazen, or they were so hungry, that they were no longer afraid of people. The old man stamped his boots down in the corner several times. Basya had leapt to her feet and stood in the centre of the cell, her body blocking the lighter square of the window. She was trembling with fright.

'They bite. They were nibbling my feet. I'm so frightened of them.'

'Don't worry. Don't be afraid. Rats, so what? Rats aren't frightening. They bite, but so what? That's nothing compared to real troubles. Come on, you sit in my corner, and I'll stay here. I'll keep them away.'

He stamped a few more times, turned back to the corner and sat down. Basya curled into the place on the straw that he had left. Sotnikov appeared to be asleep. Over on the other side, Demchikha was sighing, and occasionally blowing her nose.

'Now, what do we do now?' Pyotr asked in the darkness, and answered himself: 'There's nothing we can do. Just wait. There's not long left.'

It grew quiet again. Rybak stretched his legs more easily and wanted to go to sleep, but sleep wouldn't come.

There was a precipice ahead of him.

He knew that very clearly, particularly now, in the night, in the moment of stillness, and he realised there was nothing he could do about it. Always before he had managed to find a way out, but not now. Now there was no way out. Despite himself, he felt his fear growing, as it had that time in his childhood, when fear had overcome his childish reason. That had been a long time ago, before collectivisation, when he was a child in the village—why should he remember it now? But for some reason it had come into his memory, unwilling to recall it though he was. It was as if that far-off event had some still unclear connection with his present situation.

They lived in the village, no worse off or better off than the others. They were just about average. His father had a well-made bay horse, young and hard working, a little on the fiery side, although young Kolya Rybak could cope with him perfectly well. In the village the children started learning the peasants' work early in life, and before he was twelve Kolya had already begun to learn to reap and plough and harrow.

That day they were bringing the sheaves home from the fields.

That was work entirely fitted to a child. He knew the road well, every detail was engraved on his mind. He could remember with his eyes closed where the cart had to go a little on one side, where it was best to keep in the ruts, where it was best to ford the channel of deep water where the road dipped. The most dangerous place on the road was Kuptsov hill—there was a steep hillside, and the road turned sharply round a narrow ravine with a steep drop into the valley. There you had to watch both sides of the cart. But everything was going well. His father forked the last two sheaves on to the top of the load—the cart looked over-full, there was only just enough rope to tie the load on. Kolya sat on top with his seven-year-old sister Manya and their neighbour's daughter Lyuba.

He rode quietly on top of the load the whole way, swaying from side to side, controlling the horse with his usual complete confidence. They were passing Kuptsov hill, and the road was going down into the dip. Then suddenly something happened to the reins and he couldn't hold the horse. The left hand side of the cart reared up and the whole thing began to tilt to the right. Kolya glanced down and went cold with fright.

Probably he should have turned the outfit sharply to the left, and then they might have managed to stay on the edge of the drop, but he was too afraid to realise this simple way out. Terrified, Kolya jumped down from the cart, which was beginning to slip down the side of the precipice dragging the horse with it, and the little girls sitting on top of the load.

When he picked himself up, he didn't even look down after it, but ran over the grass to the alder trees. Afraid of his father's anger, he wandered in the forest until sunset. Contrary to his expectations, his father didn't beat him, didn't even tell him off as much as he might have—it wasn't worth the trouble. The neighbour's daughter had a broken arm, the axle of the cart was broken and the horse stood gloomily in the yard, one bandaged leg held off the ground.

Afterwards he was criticised in the village, and he himself knew that he had been wrong to jump from the cart, but he still didn't know what would have happened if he had stayed on it. Probably he would have fallen under the cart and might not have escaped with his life. Many years had passed since that time, but he still couldn't be sure what would have been the correct course of action.

Now once again he faced a precipice.

But this time there was no chance of jumping off the cart, because now Rybak was fastened on with a rope, and to make sure that he didn't untie himself, they had set guards over him.

But surely the investigator couldn't have been lying when he promised him whatever it was, almost persuaded him? It was probably a pity Rybak hadn't agreed straight away—tomorrow might be too late. But that was understandable—the investigator probably wasn't the real boss round here, there must be a higher

140

authority. They had issued an order, and that was that. And it was probably too late to correct anything, to change anything.

No, he would not accept death, he would not take it meekly and humbly. He would tear their *politsai* limb from limb, and strangle Portnov and that Stas with his bare hands. If only they would let him get at them . . .

16

After his conversation with the headman, which totally exhausted him although it was so brief, Sotnikov slept for a short time. When he woke he found he was soaked in sweat. The fever that had been burning him up for so long had given place to a sweaty chill, and Sotnikov huddled shivering beneath his long greatcoat. But his head felt clearer; the febrile stupor which had clouded it had lifted, and he felt a great deal better. Had it not been for his mutilated swollen fingers and his leg which still throbbed with the old pain, he might have accounted himself fit.

It was dark and quiet in the cellar, but it seemed that no one was asleep—or at least so he judged from the frequent sighs, movements and cautious quiet breathing of the people about him. Then Sotnikov suddenly remembered that they were living out their last night of life, and that tomorrow would not be theirs.

So he felt he had to gather and husband his remaining strength so that he could face death honourably. Of course, he had expected nothing better from these traitors. Of course they couldn't keep him alive—all they could do was torture him in Budila's devilish workshop. So perhaps it wasn't a bad thing after all. A bullet cuts life off instantly and without pain—not the worst of all possible deaths, and of course a soldier's normal death in time of war.

Yet, he, fool, had always been afraid of dying in battle. Now a death like that with a gun in his hands seemed an unattainable luxury, and he almost envied those thousands of lucky men who had met an honourable end in the front line. Every time that he had emerged in the past from a front line battle he had felt a quiet satisfaction that the bullets had passed him by. But what had those few extra months of life given him, crammed full as they had been of daily terrors, cold, discomfort, and hunger, and which were now drawing near to their end, the usual end in war—death.

It was true that during his months as a partisan he had managed to get something done, he had carried out his duty as a citizen and a soldier. Perhaps not as he would have wished, but as circumstances allowed. A few of the enemy had met their death at his hands. That was the only consolation, the only good reason for his twenty-six years of life—he could find no other justification at all. Indeed, what other good had he contributed to people's lives? He had planted no trees, dug no wells, killed no serpents—without which, according to the Eastern proverb, a life lived on earth is of no value.

So the end had come.

And when he died, as far as he was concerned everything he knew would die with him—the whole huge world, with its past, present and future, would disappear into limbo. He knew, of course, that the world would go on, and even if it wasn't losing much with the loss of one insignificant life, which although it might have had the capacity to enrich the world, had never implemented that capacity in any way whatsoever, he, Sotnikov, was losing everything with no hope of ever gaining anything.

But now, a few hours before the end, to his own surprise he began to discover within himself some new sensations which he previously had been unaware of. First of all he lost the uncertainty which had dogged him for long months through the war, when even the most immediate future was clouded in the mists of the unknowable. Now everything was clear and categorical. So as not to console himself with empty hopes, he shook off one after another all the illusions he had held in life, and knew that ahead there lay nothing. In a way this was a relief, because it gave him the opportunity to limit severely his choice of action. If anything now remained in life to concern him, it was only his final responsibilities towards the people around him. He knew that it would not be right to die before clarifying his relationships with them, since those relationships would be the final manifestation of his ego before it finally vanished.

Once he had come to terms with his own death, for a few hours he achieved a strange, almost absolute independence from the strength of his enemies. Now that he had abandoned all hope of preserving his own life he felt able to indulge other more altruistic ideas. He felt that he had gained a new opportunity, which could not be suppressed by the enemy, nor by circumstances, nor by anyone in the world. Since he was afraid of nothing, he had a clear

143

advantage over the others, and over his former self as well. Of course this was the advantage of a dead man, but at the same time it seemed the main, and perhaps the only real value in his essentially insignificant life. He realised that he could get no personal benefit from it, but perhaps there was still something he could do for those close to him. And Sotnikov took the last decision that was open to him: to take everything on himself. The decision came easily and with a clear logic. Tomorrow he would tell the interrogator that he had been on a reconnaissance, that he had a certain mission, that he had wounded the *politsai* in an exchange of fire, that he was an officer in the Red Army and an enemy of fascism, and let them shoot him. The others had nothing to do with it at all.

In fact he was sacrificing himself in order to save the others, but his self-sacrifice was as necessary to him as it was to them. It was no matter of naive illusions—Sotnikov could not accept that his death was a mere ridiculous coincidence carried out at the will of these drunken traitors. Like every death in battle, his death had to affirm some values and reject others, and as far as possible reach a climax that in life he had not been able to achieve. Otherwise, what was the point of life? Life is too great a trial for its end to be faced without due consideration.

It was quite cold, and from time to time he shivered and pulled his coat more closely about him. As always it was a relief to have made a decision, and the most exhausting thing about war—the uncertainty—no longer nagged at his mind. He already knew when his last battle with the enemy was to take place, and he knew what position he was going to adopt. And he would not abandon that position. And although this single combat held out hopes of no easy victory, yet he was calm. The Germans and their friends had the weapons, the strength, but he too had something to support him to the end. He was not afraid of them.

The greatcoat about him brought some warmth back, and he fell asleep again.

And he dreamed a strange confused dream.

It was more than a little surprising that he could dream such a dream on the last night of his life. He dreamt of things from his childhood, and among other things of a stupid episode which involved his father's Mauser. It seemed that Sotnikov took the gun from its holster, swung it carelessly to one side and broke the barrel, which turned out to be made not of metal but of tin, like that of a toy pistol. Sotnikov was terrified, although in the dream he was not a child, but almost his present age, or at least a student—the dream was taking place in the armoury at his college. He stood beside the rifle-rack and wondered what to do; his father was due to arrive at any moment. Sotnikov rushed to the rack, but there wasn't a single empty space—there was a rifle in every slot. Then with shaking fingers he wrenched open the metal door of the stove and thrust the pistol into the black, ash-filled cavity.

The next moment a fire leapt up in the stove—a white hot, sparkling coal fire, in the midst of which it looked as if something bright was melting, and in utter confusion he stood and watched, not knowing what to do. His father stood behind him. The older Sotnikov did not even mention the Mauser, although his son felt that he knew everything that had just happened. Then his father squatted down on his haunches in front of the stove and said, apparently regretfully, in a lisping, old man's voice, 'There was a fire, and it was the greatest justice on earth . . .'

It seemed to Sotnikov that that came from the Bible, that thick book in the black embossed binding that had lain in the past on his mother's dressing table. As a child he had sometimes leafed through its yellow pages, which gave out a special strange smell of old books. Now he was surprised to hear his father quoting the Bible, as he did not believe in God, and had had an open dislike of priests.

Sotnikov did not know how long that fire burnt, for his dream faded again into a dark mist. But it was probably some time before he came to himself, and began to be aware of some nearby sounds—a bang, a rustling of straw, and the quiet voice of an old man. When he got back to reality, Sotnikov realised that they had been chasing a rat away. When he was fully awake, he lay and coughed painfully for some time, trying to work out what his dream could have meant. And gradually and naturally his thoughts returned to a melancholy memory of his earliest, furthest childhood . . .

The Mauser was not an object that he had purely dreamt up. It really had belonged to his father, a former Red Army officer, and before that an ensign in the Tsarist Army with two St. George's crosses on his chest—he had once seen a photograph of his father in officer's uniform in his mother's beautiful red treasure box, with its decoration of peacocks. Sometimes, on holidays, his father would take his Mauser from the sideboard drawer, and his son held the yellow wooden holster. It was difficult to draw the gun out, as the butt, which had been damaged during the war, was gradually becoming detached. Those were the happiest moments in the boy's life, but he was only allowed to watch his father draw the gun—he was not once allowed to handle it himself. 'It is forbidden to play with guns and medals,' his father would say, and the boy never pressed the point, never asked to be allowed. In the family the father's word was law, and his will reigned in everything great and small. No one found this at all strange. His father was well known in the town—even perhaps famous—as a hero of the Civil War, and only earned his living as a watchmaker—as Sotnikov's mother once explained to him—because of his war wound and his pride.

The blue steel Mauser in the wooden holster was the secret dream of the boy Sotnikov, but it was no use asking even his mother if he could play with it. So one day he decided to take it himself.

One morning he woke up early. The house was very quiet. His father seemed to have left his workroom, from where the usual sound of clock mechanisms flowed through the house, and his mother, he knew, had gone off to church—the clangour of bells for early service rang over the town.

He hurriedly pulled on his shorts, left washing and teeth cleaning till later, and slipped swiftly into his mother's bedroom. The sacred drawer of the dressing table was locked, but the small brass key was in the keyhole. The boy gave it one turn, and took out the smooth, lacquered unexpectedly heavy holster. On its wooden side there was the familiar plate with the inscription which he knew by heart: 'To Red Army Squadron Commander A. Sotnikov from the Revolutionary Military Soviet of the Cavalry Army'. The boy was excited by his first touch of the wood inlaid fretted butt. His hands coped readily with the catch on the holster, and then the whole Mauser slowly but obediently emerged from the holster, its blue steel parts glinting dully and secretly. A feeling of terrified excitement such as he had never felt before gripped the boy, and for a moment he merely examined the gun. He moved the sight, tried to open the breech, looked down the barrel. But of course the greatest delight was to aim the weapon. He had only just managed to get his hand round the butt and squeeze the trigger when totally unexpectedly and incomprehensibly a shot rang out somewhere under the table.

For a moment he stood as if turned to stone, his ears ringing

146

painfully with the sound. Plaster from the wall had flaked off on to the floor, and under the table—where it had come from he couldn't make out—was a thick piece of wood with the dark mark of the bullet lying across it.

When he finally realised what had happened, he thrust the Mauser back into its holster, pushed it into the dressing table drawer, and waited anxiously for his mother to come home. When she did, she was immediately aware that something had gone wrong, showered her son with questions, and he told her everything just as it had happened. Of course she couldn't deal with a tragedy of this magnitude herself. She was a little afraid of her husband, and burst into tears, which had never happened before, and told him that he must confess everything to his father.

It wasn't easy to screw himself up to this confession. It took more than an hour for him to get his courage up, but finally he apprehensively pushed open the door of his father's workshop.

His father was working. As always he was bent low over the bench under the window, poking about in the inside of a clock. His right hand in its black glove rested uselessly on his knee, while the left skilfully tapped, screwed, picked up and fitted together all the tiny shining parts which go to make up a clock. On the walls pendulums swung out of time with one another. A couple of dozen cheap clocks with unpainted faces, and a few alarm clocks, tinkled and ticked on a shelf, and in the corner there stood a huge weight-driven case clock which had been brought in the previous day from the town hall. His father did not turn round as the son entered, but he recognised his footstep unfailingly, and said, entirely inappropriately for the situation:

'Well, young man, how are you getting on? Have you finished the sea stories?'

The boy swallowed the lump which had suddenly come into his throat—the previous day he had started to read Stanyukovich. He had read nearly all the books which lay in his grandfather's trunk, except for the collected works of Pisemsky and a few volumes of Stanyukovich, one of which his father had chosen for him the day before yesterday. But now he couldn't talk about books, and he said:

'Papa, I took your Mauser.'

His father shook his head strangely, laid down his pincers, took his glasses off with a familiar gesture, and looked sternly at his son.

147

'Who gave you permission?'

'No one ... And it ... it went off,' his son forced himself to admit, in a small voice.

His father said nothing more, just got up and left the room. Young Sotnikov stood waiting by the door feeling as if he ought to go off and put his head under the blade of a guillotine. But he knew that he was guilty, and was ready to accept the most pitiless punishment.

Soon his father came back.

'You young puppy!' he said, as he came in. 'What right did you have to touch a weapon without permission? How dare you open that drawer like a thief?'

His father lectured him long and pitilessly—for carelessness, for the shot, which might have hurt someone, and most of all for his secret disobedience.

'The only thing that softens your guilt is that you confessed. Only that saves you. Do you understand?'

'Yes.'

'Of course, if you thought of it for yourself. Yourself?'

His son, feeling that he would be struck down, nodded, and his father let out a long, relieved sigh.

'Well, thank you for that.'

That was too much—to win his father's thanks with an unwanted lie—and his eyes clouded and blood rushed to his face. He stood unable to move.

'Go and play,' his father said.

So on the whole he got away with the encounter lightly—he'd avoided a beating, but that spineless nod stayed lodged in his soul like a painful splinter. It was a lesson that lasted him all his life. He never again lied to his father or to anyone else. He always kept his promises, and looked people in the eye. Of course, his mother never told his father on whose initiative the confession had been made. And so this cavalry officer, pensioner of the Civil War, and master clock repairer finished his earthly life happily convinced of his son's honesty, and hoping that his son would find something better in life than he had himself.

Well, now he had found it ...

17

The sleepy silence of the early morning was broken by footsteps, the muffled sound of voices and the slamming of doors. Here in the cellar the door slams sounded especially loud, so much so that occasionally a particularly heavy slam brought dust showering from the ceiling. Rybak was not asleep—he lay on his side against the wall, his legs folded under him, and listened, listened with total concentration. The window high in the wall became a little lighter—it was probably full daylight outside by now, and it was becoming easier to make things out in the cell. The indistinct, crumpled figures of the prisoners emerged slowly from the darkness of night—opposite him Demchikha, who had calmed down by now; in the corner Pyotr sat motionless, his face deep in gloom. Basya could not yet be seen in the darkness of the wall below the window. Sotnikov was still lying on his back beside Rybak, breathing noisily. If it hadn't been for that breathing, he could easily have been taken for dead. A difficult day, perhaps their last, was beginning, and they were anticipating it and holding their peace, each living through his torment alone.

The footsteps overhead became more frequent, and the door slammed constantly. Then suddenly a conversation in the yard came through to the cellar. Rybak raised his head, and turned on one side, towards the wall. He couldn't make out the words, but it was clear that people were gathering in the yard, perhaps forming up for parade. But why had no one come down into the cellar yet? It looked as if they had been forgotten.

Someone walked along by the wall outside, and the prisoners could hear his boots squeaking in the snow. There was a clang of metal somewhere near the window, and a rough, coarse voice said:

'There are three here altogether.'

'And there was a shovel as well. Look for the shovel.'

'A shovel's no use! It's spades we need!'

There was another metallic clang, the footsteps went away, and everything grew quiet again. But Rybak had been shaken by that short exchange. Why spades? The only use spades had was for digging, and what digging was there to do in the middle of winter? A trench? A ditch? Perhaps a grave—but for whom?

And then he remembered: perhaps that *politsai* had died.

He looked questioningly around. Demchikha looked at him, alarmed and uncomprehending from below her crumpled head-scarf. Pyotr sat motionless in his corner in tense anticipation. No one spoke a word, they were all listening, gripped by terror and uncertainty.

But they were not left uncertain for long. Shortly there were more footsteps along the wall, but this time so firm and definite that now no one had any doubts—this time they were coming for them in the cellar. When the first door squeaked open, Rybak sat up abruptly, his heart pounding. Beside him Sotnikov moved, and began to cough. When they open the door, rush them, knock them over, and out through the door, thought Rybak, but realised immediately that there wasn't a chance, with stairs just beyond the door.

By this time the door was already swinging open. The cold air from outside hit them, morning fresh and the dim light from outside illuminated the five grey, frightened faces. The efficient Stas appeared in the doorway, with someone else carrying a rifle behind him.

'That's enough sleep!' The *politsai* bawled at the top of his voice. 'That's all the sleep you're getting. Get outside—liquidation!'

So we weren't mistaken, this really is the end, passed through Rybak's mind. If they're going to kill one, that goes for all of us. For a moment he slumped, as if every last dreg of strength had drained away, then he wearily gathered in his legs, set his hat on his head, and only then pressed his hands against the straw trying to get to his feet.

'Jump to it!' Stas urged them noisily. Pyotr was the first to get to his feet, groaning slightly, and Demchikha began to rise. Sotnikov got up with immense difficulty, pulling himself up the wall. Rybak looked unseeingly at his white, lined, sleep-starved face, his eyes set in dark hollows, and tried to speak but found he could think of nothing to say and walked to the door.

150

'Come on, come on! There's only twenty minutes left,' the *politsai* bawled at them, stepping in to their stinking straw-strewn cell. 'You, one-legged, get moving!'

'Keep your hands off! I'll manage on my own!' snarled Sotnikov.

'And you, Jewess, what are you waiting for? Shift, will you! Didn't want to confess, but she'll talk on the end of a rope!' Stas thought that was a huge joke, but then turned savage again, 'Get out of it, filthy Jew!'

They climbed the snow-covered concrete steps to the yard. Rybak moved his feet wearily. He hadn't fastened his coat, but he didn't notice the biting cold of the frost. After a night in the foul-smelling cellar, his head swam from the fresh air as if from liquor. Across the yard from them was a line of six *politsai* with their weapons at the ready—they were waiting. It was a gloomy morning with a light frost, and blue clouds of smoke poured from the chimneys up above the roofs into the sky.

Rybak paused uncertainly in front of the porch. Demchikha came to a halt beside him, and Basya huddled up to her as if she were her mother. She looked terrified at the *politsai* as she stood there, pressing her shivering soaking bare feet together. Pyotr stood morosely aloof looking like a grey-haired patriarch. Meanwhile Stas, a stream of obscenities flowing from him, lugged Sotnikov up the steps, and heaved him into the snow as soon as he reached the top. Sotnikov gave himself no time to rest, but dragged himself to his feet and stood erect in his creased, blood-stained greatcoat.

'Where is the interrogator? Call the interrogator!' he tried to shout in a muffled, tearing voice, and began to cough. Rybak suddenly thought that he too needed to see the interrogator, but unlike Sotnikov, he spoke calmly:

'Yes, take us to the interrogator. He said yesterday that he would see me again.'

'We'll take you, all right,' a thickset, heavy faced *politsai* jeered, as he approached with a rope in his hands. 'Let's have your hands.'

There was nothing he could do. Rybak held out his hands and the *politsai* grabbed them and with one skilful movement whipped them behind his back and began to tie them while one of his colleagues held them. All this was done unceremoniously, coarsely and brutally. Rybak winced—not so much from the pain in his wrists, but from the despair which was enveloping him; this really was the end of everything.

151

'Tell the interrogator. We must see the interrogator,' he said, but not very firmly, as he was beginning to feel the ground giving way beneath his feet. The *politsai* behind him merely bellowed angrily:

'It's too late. The case is closed.'

'What d'you mean, closed?' shouted Rybak, and looked back over his shoulder. He saw an unshaven jaw, thick in white stubble, close-set pig-like eyes, which showed complete indifference towards him—it wouldn't be easy to frighten a man like that. Then Rybak took the only course now open to him, and began to ask instead of order:

'Go on, call Portnov. What difference does it make to you? Are you men or aren't you?'

But Portnov, it seemed, was further away than Rybak's own death. No one even answered him.

Meanwhile they had finished tying his hands skilfully and tightly with a thin rope, which bit painfully into his skin, and he was thrust aside. They moved on to Demchikha.

'You, bring the interrogator here!' Sotnikov demanded coldly of Stas through a burst of coughing, while Stas, his rifle slung over his shoulder, was busying himself with Demchikha. But Stas didn't even look at him, and like everyone else seemed to be deaf to their requests, as if they had already ceased to be people. This convinced Rybak still more firmly that everything was over. They were going to die. But how could that be? And why hadn't he made his mind up while his hands were still free?

Something inside him turned over at his recognition that he was totally powerless and he looked distractedly around him. But there was no hope of salvation. Indeed, judging by everything that was going on, their end was growing rapidly nearer. One by one the senior ranks were filing out on to the porch—some officers in new uniforms that had obviously only just been issued to them—short black greatcoats with grey collars and cuffs, and pistols in their belts; two, probably Germans, in long greatcoats with high-peaked caps. A few men in civilian clothes, with scarves round their necks, stood noticeably apart, as if they were guests invited to some alien festival. The *politsai* in the yard grew respectfully hushed, and fell into line. Behind the prisoners someone hurriedly counted, 'One, two, three, four, five.'

'Is everything ready?' a broad-shouldered *politsai* with a small holster on his stomach asked from the porch. It was the holster, and an air of strength and of domination over the rest, that suggested to Rybak that this was the head man. He had just thought of this when Sotnikov, standing behind him, shouted hoarsely:

'Sir, I want to say something.'

The chief stopped stock still on the steps, and turned his heavy eyes on the prisoner.

'What's that?'

'I am a partisan. It was I who wounded your *politsai*,' Sotnikov said quite quietly. He nodded towards Rybak. 'This man here was there merely by chance—if you wish I can explain. The rest have absolutely nothing to do with any of this. Take me and leave them.'

The officers on the porch stopped chatting, and two of them stepped forward exchanging puzzled looks, and Rybak felt a tiny spark of possible salvation grow in his mind, setting light to a weak hope: Might they believe Sotnikov? And this hopeful feeling made him quietly grateful to Sotnikov.

But the momentary attention on the face of the chief gave way to impatient severity.

'Is that all?' he asked coldly, and stepped down into the snow.

The unexpectedness of the reply left Sotnikov tongue-tied for a moment.

'I can explain in greater detail.'

Someone growled discontentedly, there were a few muttered words in German, and the chief waved his hand.

'Take them away!'

Rybak retreated into despair. They don't even want to listen, he thought. Probably everything had been decided well before. But where did that leave him? Surely Sotnikov's heroic intercession could not fail to save him?

The *politsai* were filing down from the porch now, stepping gingerly on the creaking wooden stairs. Suddenly Rybak recognised one of them as Portnov, this time wearing the *politsai* uniform. Of course, that was yesterday's interrogator, who had given him so much hope with his proposal, and who now seemed to have retracted. When he saw him, Rybak started, and pushed forward. Whatever happened, now he was afraid of nothing, and didn't even find it difficult.

'Mr. Interrogator! Mr. Interrogator! A moment please! I'll agree to what you said yesterday. I swear I had nothing to do with this. You heard what he said . . .'

153

The officers, who were already going out of the yard into the street, began to stop one by one. They again looked displeased. Portnov stopped too. His new police greatcoat obviously did not fit him and hung in stiff folds on his small thin body, and his black forage cap was set on one side like a cock's comb. But there was no doubt that the uniform gave the interrogator a kind of magisterial importance, a kind of showy severity. A tall, tightly belted German in a greatcoat looked inquiringly at Portnov, and the interrogator briskly explained something in German.

'Very well. Untie him!'

'Swine!' the quiet, bitter word struck him like a blow in the back of the neck. It was Sotnikov, of course, as the familiar painful cough confirmed.

But let him say what he liked. Something awful which had been moving on him inexorably had been halted and was now suddenly receding. Rybak breathed deeper, and felt his hands being untied behind his back. But he didn't even look round. He was aware of only one thing—he was going to live! His unbound hands fell to his sides of their own accord, and again without being aware of what he was doing he took a step to the side, trying with all his being to get away from the others—now he wanted to be as far away from them as possible. He moved another three paces, and no one stopped him. One of the officers turned away towards the gate, when Demchikha shouted behind him:

'Ah, you've let him go! Then let me go! Let me free! I'll tell you who hid her! That one there! I'll tell! I've got children, and God knows what's happening to them!'

Her cry, filled with wild despair, brought everyone to a standstill, and the nearest to her was Portnov. The tall German looked annoyed and rapped out a few words, and the interrogator went over to the woman.

'Well, who was it then?'

'Untie me!'

'Tarasyuk!' Portnov called.

The *politsai* who had tied Rybak's hands hurried up to Demchikha and freed her hands from the rope. She stood in confusion rubbing her hands on the skirts of her coat. But the *politsai* and the Germans were waiting.

'Well, where was she hiding?' Portnov prompted her.

'With that man, what do they call him . . .'

154

'You're talking rubbish,' Pyotr interrupted, quietly but firmly. 'Think on God.'

'It was . . . it was with Fyodor Burak, I think.'

'What, Burak?' frowned Portnov. 'Burak left here long ago. You'll have to do better than that.'

Demchikha went stubborn and didn't speak.

'Well?'

'I've told you.'

'Tarasyuk!'

'You're lying.'

Tarasyuk, who was standing ready behind the woman, understood perfectly, and grabbed her by the arms.

'But I told you! I told you!' screamed Demchikha heartrendingly. 'May you be struck by lightening! What are you doing? I've got children! I've got three children at home.'

'Shut up you bitch!' the *politsai* barked, twisting her arms pitilessly behind her. Demchikha screamed and struggled, but it was soon over, and he pushed her away.

'Ready!'

'Take them away!' said Portnov, and turned to Rybak. 'You give him a hand!' he said, pointing to Sotnikov.

Rybak didn't like this idea. From now on he wanted to keep as far away from Sotnikov as he could. But an order's an order, and he went willingly to his former comrade and took him by the arm.

They were led out into the street through the wide open gates. *Politsai* with rifles at the ready marched on either side. The straggling group of officers lagged behind, allowing the prisoners and their escort to go on ahead. Pyotr went first—tall and old, his white head bare, and his arms wrenched behind him. Then came Demchikha, dragging herself along, sobbing bitterly in her hopeless despair. And beside her walked Basya, her bare feet showing beneath a dark coloured long sleeved garment clearly not her own.

Rybak held Sotnikov by the arm. He seemed to have shrunk, his face was even more drawn, and he dragged slowly along after the others, coughing, and limping heavily on his wounded leg. His foot was turning black and trailed its toes in the snow, leaving strange tracks behind. He did not speak, and Rybak could not summon up courage to speak to him. As they went along together they were on opposite sides of the line which separates friends from enemies. Although Rybak felt that he was guilty of something, nevertheless

155

he tried to convince himself that he bore no great guilt. A guilty man is one who does something of his own free and evil will, or for gain, and what did he stand to gain? It was just that he had had a better chance, and he had used his cunning to give himself an opportunity of getting out of it alive. But he was no traitor. At all events he had no intention of serving the Germans. He was just waiting for the right moment to come along—it could be now, it could be later, and he would see it when it came.

18

Sotnikov began to understand more and more clearly that he had gained absolutely nothing. His idea of taking all the blame on himself, which had almost brought him calm and peace, had collapsed. It was plain that he had overestimated his own strength in this duel, and had underestimated the perfidy of his enemies. Of course, the *politsai* were puppets in the hands of the Germans, and that was why they had remained so totally indifferent to what he had told them—it didn't matter a damn to them who was guilty, if they had had an order to kill someone.

Suffering cruelly from the pain in his leg, Sotnikov was barely able to keep up with the others, and he tried not to lean too heavily on Rybak's arm—now an alien, hateful arm. Of course people could commit any betrayal from fear or from hate, but Rybak had not seemed to be either a traitor or a coward. No matter how many chances of joining the police he had been offered, and there had been plenty of opportunities for cowardice, he had always behaved decently, and certainly no worse than the others. But when it came to the point, it seemed that he was lacking in something—determination, perhaps, or principle. Or maybe when it came down to brass tacks, the whole thing was done merely to save his own skin—a pressure that always leads to treachery. But in the last analysis there is something in this world incomparably more important than one's own skin.

Now Sotnikov was bitterly ashamed at his naive fantasy—having given into such a stupid fantasy—that he, having lost all hope of saving his own life, could do something to save the others. But are people who will pay any price to save their own lives worth even one life given for them? How many human lives since the time of Jesus Christ had been laid on the sacrificial altar of humanity, and yet had humanity learnt anything from them? Just as thousands of years ago, so today; man is still primarily concerned with himself, and any attempt at self-sacrifice is seen as at best eccentric, and at worst the stupidity of a dreamer.

Gradually Sótnikov mastered his feelings, and as he did so he became aware of the cold. His weakness had brought a sweat out on his forehead, and it slowly dried out in the freezing wind, the cold making his head throb and ache deep in his brain. The bitter wind finally drove any remaining shreds of warmth from his body and he began to shake and tremble with fever again. But Sotnikov was determined to hold out to the end.

They walked along the deserted street, crossed a bridge, and continued into a small square surrounded by buildings, with a few rows of meagre trees frozen in the wind. Ahead of them on a low rise stood a white two-storeyed house, with the broad banner of the fascist flag flying from the corner. It was probably the H.Q. of the Kommandatura, and close by a small crowd of people stood dark against the snow. Sotnikov was surprised, and wondered what had made all these people come together in one place. Perhaps it was market day today? Or perhaps something had happened? Or, most likely of all, the population had been forced to come here to witness the execution and be duly terrified. If that was what it was, then let them be shot now—it would be easier to face death in public. As far as terrifying people goes, there is terror to spare in wars, but that doesn't stop battles from taking place. Other people come in to replace the fallen. There are always brave men to be found.

They slowly approached the house. Sotnikov's leg, like an unbending artificial limb, carved strange holes in the soft snow, marked already by sleigh runners and hoofmarks, and it burnt with a constant depth of pain. He was able to make it obey him only by a great effort of will—now he was almost hanging on Rybak's strong arm. Once they were over the bridge the road began to rise gently, and it became even harder for him to keep going. He couldn't breathe, his vision darkened, and the road kept slipping from beneath his feet. He was afraid that he wouldn't make it, that he would fall and be shot where he lay, like a dog in a ditch. No, he couldn't allow that to happen—even in his situation that would be too much. Whatever death he was to suffer, he felt he must meet it like a soldier, with honour. That had become the main aim of his last moments.

They came to the top of the slope and stopped. Breathing

158

heavily, Sotnikov gazed at the back of those ahead of him, waiting for them to move off again. But the escorting *politsai* had also stopped, and he heard a conversation in German from out in front—a few officers were waiting along the wall of the solid building. Opposite across the street by the fence enclosing the square, near two rickety market stalls, five or six dozen people stood in the cold, clearly waiting for something. It looked as if the small procession had reached its destination—there was no road beyond this point.

And then Sotnikov saw the nooses.

Five supple hempen nooses swayed quietly above the street, as if to show everyone the high quality of their skilfully prepared knots. They hung from the cross piece of an old, pre-war arch. They've found a use for it, thought Sotnikov, despite himself. He had seen arches just like this one in many regional towns. There had been one exactly like it in his own home town. Before the main holidays— May Day and the anniversary of the Revolution—the arch was decorated with birch and pine branches, and a slogan hung from the top, written in ink on pieces of wall paper. Nearby, outside the regional executive committee offices, there were special meetings with speeches, and the children from the two schools, the workers from the flax factory, the workshops and the packaging mill formed up in columns to pass under the low arch. Usually there would be a plywood star fastened over the cross beam or a flag blowing in the wind. Now there was nothing, except for a few scraps of paper clinging to the blackened laths of the uprights, and an odd tattered piece of rag the size of the corner of a neckerchief fluttering in the wind. The occupiers had decorated the arch after their own fashion with these new nooses, probably specially drawn from the stores against an event like this.

And he had thought they would be shot . . .

Two men, a *politsai* and someone in a long grey cloth coat were carrying an old rickety bench across the street, and Sotnikov realised that this was for them—so that they could reach the nooses before they dangled there, their heads over one shoulder, ugly and voiceless. He was suddenly disgusted by the mere thought of himself hanged, and by the whole of this degrading, inhuman massacre. Throughout the war the thought of dying otherwise than from a bullet or from shrapnel had never occurred to him, and everything in him revolted in instinctive protest against the devilish suffocation by the noose.

But there was no way in which he could help himself or the others. He merely kept on trying to persuade himself, it doesn't matter, it doesn't matter! When it came down to it, they had the right, the power, to exercise this bestial practice. Now his last obligation was to endure, without any sign of fear or regret. Let them hang him.

They seemed to have got the bench in position. The efficient, omnipresent Stas, the huge tightly belted Budila, and the other *politsai* began to lead them to the arch. Limping on his rigidly frozen painful leg, Sotnikov waited until they were fifteen or twenty paces away, and then shook his arm free of Rybak's grasp. He wanted to go alone. They went past the *politsai*, past the group of German and civilian senior staff, who were patiently waiting, stamping their feet, along the wall of the building. The show was about to begin—police amateur dramatics German style. The *politsai* hurried busily about, getting anxious. It looked as if something had gone wrong. Some of the officers were frowning, while others chatted among themselves in a relaxed, easy manner, as if they had met for a routine, not particularly interesting but necessary purpose, and would soon be going back to their normal day's work. An aroma of cigarette-smoke and eau-de-cologne drifted over from them, and there were snatches of disconnected, meaningless phrases. But Sotnikov was not looking in their direction—once he had dragged himself to the arch, he leant his shoulder against one of the uprights so as not to fall, and closed his eyes in exhaustion.

No, death certainly resolved nothing and justified nothing. Only life gives people a definite opportunity, which they either make something of or waste completely, only life can stand up to evil and violence. Death is deprived of everything. And if that lieutenant in the pine grove had managed to accomplish something by the manner of his death, he could hardly have intended the effect he produced. It was merely that a death like that was necessary for him, because he did not want to go like a lamb to the slaughter. But what can you do when no matter how determined you are you haven't got the slightest opportunity to do anything about it? What can you do five minutes before the end, when you are already barely alive, and you aren't even in a condition to curse and shout loudly so as to anger your captors?

Yes, there would be no reward, as there would be no gratitude, for there is no point in hoping for what is not deserved. Yet he could not agree with Rybak's action, which contradicted his entire humanity, his faith and his moral code. And although his already limited number of opportunities was diminishing still further, and even death could do nothing to increase it, there was still one possibility open to him. And from that possibility he would not shrink. That possibility, the only one, depended on him and on no one else. Only he was fully in command of it, since it lay in his power alone to leave the world according to his conscience, with a dignity worthy of a man. This was the last grace accorded him, a holy luxury, which life had awarded him as it might have been a decoration.

One by one they were led under the gallows. Under the noose furthest from the group of officers they put Pyotr, quiet, submissive and withdrawn. Sotnikov looked at him and frowned guiltily. Yesterday he had been angry that they had not shot the headman, and now he had to hang with him from the same gibbet. They made Pyotr get up on the bench first. It wobbled threateningly as he knelt on it, and almost tipped over. Budila, who seemed to be the chief executioner, swore, climbed on the bench and hauled the old man up alongside him. The headman cautiously stood erect on the bench, his head lowered, and bowed to the people, a restrained, meaningful bow, as in a church. Then they pushed Basya under the arch. She climbed up to her place submissively, and stood there, shifting from one cold chapped foot to the other, and with childlike simplicity gazed at the crowd by the fence as if she was trying to find someone she knew. But the bench was not long enough for all of them. Under the next noose a plywood packing case had been placed, and in the next two places there were newly sawn sections of a tree trunk, a foot and a half high. Sotnikov thought that the packing case was intended for him, but they took Demchikha to it, and Rybak and a *politsai* took him to the end to one of the logs.

He still hadn't reached his place when he heard Demchikha cry out behind him. He turned his head involuntarily—the woman had dug her heels in and was resisting the *politsai* with all her strength, refusing to let herself be led beneath the noose.

'Oh, forgive me! Forgive a stupid woman, I didn't want anything, I didn't realise!'

Her wailing was drowned by the angry shouts of the officers, Budila gave an order, and the *politsai* who was leading Sotnikov left him to Rybak and hurled himself at Demchikha. Several of the *politsai* dragged her on to the packing case.

Rybak, on his own now with Sotnikov, led him uncertainly towards the last log beneath the arch, and stopped. Immediately above their heads hung the new hempen noose, new as they all were, with its neat hangman's knot, swinging quietly above them. One for the two of us, thought Sotnikov involuntarily, although it was clear that this noose was for him alone. He had to climb on the log. He paused briefly undecided, until his mind flashed a despairing message, like a curse, 'Goddamn it to hell.' Rybak was motionless. Sotnikov snapped at him, 'Hold on,' and put his good knee on the top of the log, which bore the fresh imprint of a dirty bootmark. Rybak held the log steady with both hands. To keep his balance Sotnikov lightly leant his elbow on Rybak's back, tensed himself and, gritting his teeth, somehow or other hoisted himself up.

For a moment he stood quietly, his feet close together on the narrow surface of the log. He could feel the rough noose brushing the back of his neck, bringing ice into his soul. Below him Rybak's broad sheepskin-clad back was absolutely still, while his horny hands gripped the pine log. Turned over to the other side, the bastard! Sotnikov thought viciously, almost enviously, and then had a sudden doubt—should he think of Rybak in that way? Now, in the last instants of life, he had unexpectedly lost his former conviction of his right to demand the same standards from others as he demanded of himself. Rybak was a good partisan, had certainly been an experienced sergeant in the army, but as a man and as a citizen he clearly lacked something. But how could he have filled that gap? After he had left school at twelve, he had probably read no more than a dozen or so decent books. He could hardly have reached a level of morality in his spiritual development which would allow his action to be judged by mankind's highest standards.

Beside him Demchikha was still weeping and struggling in the hands of the *politsai*, and a German in yellow gloves began to read something from a piece of paper—the sentence, maybe, or an order for the local inhabitants before the execution. His last moments of life were upon him, and Sotnikov, perched on his log, drank in thirstily the familiar view of the small town street, unremarkable, but familiar from his childhood, with its sad figures of people, the

162

young trees, the broken fence, and the ice frozen in a mound by the iron pump. Through the branches of the trees in the square he could see the flaking walls of a small church, with two faded green domes rising from its rusty, crossless roof. Some of its narrow windows had been roughly blocked up with dry, unfinished slabs of cement.

But then one of the *politsai* came along and stretched up to his noose. Unceremonious hands in grey cuffs pulled the noose down over his painfully frostbitten ears and lodged it under his chin. Well, that's that, thought Sotnikov, and looked down at the people. Nature could always bring a feeling of peace and well-being to his mind, but now he wanted to see people. He looked sadly along the uneven, wary ranks in front of him. They were mainly women, with only a few elderly men, young boys and girls—an ordinary village crowd in sheepskins, padded jackets, army cast-offs, headscarves, home-made jerseys. Among the faceless multitude his eyes fell on the thin figure of a boy of twelve or so, wearing an old army cap pulled right down over his forehead. Tightly wrapped in some odd garment, the boy had drawn his freezing hands up into his sleeves, and Sotnikov could see even from where he was that he was shivering from cold, or maybe from fright. His white sickly face was childishly fascinated, and his eyes were glued to what was going on under the gallows. It was hard to tell from here what he felt about them, but Sotnikov suddenly felt a desire that he should not think badly of them. But when Sotnikov caught his eye, he saw in it so much inconsolable grief and so much sympathy that he could not help himself from smiling at the boy, just with his eyes—don't worry, lad.

Then he stopped looking at anything, and lowered his eyes, so as not to see the hateful sight of the officers, the Germans, the interrogator Portnov, Budila and Stas. Yet he could still feel their devilish presence. It seemed that the reading of the sentence was over, there were orders in German and Russian, and suddenly he felt that the noose had acquired a life of its own as it tightened against his neck. At the other end of the gallows someone choked once, and again, and then Demchikha began to scream in complete abandon.

'Ai-ai-ai! No, No!'

But her shriek was cut off suddenly, the arch above them cracked as though in a frost, and a woman in the crowd burst into sobs. He felt immensely sad. Some inner strength which was still not exhausted urged him, too, to cry out, to shriek like

Demchikha—wild and terrible. But he forced himself to stay quiet, just his heart was clenched in a pre-death convulsion; just before the end he longed to let all the brakes go and weep. Instead of which he suddenly smiled for the last time—a sad, tortured smile.

There was an order from one of the officers, which clearly referred to him. The log beneath his feet teetered for a second. Sotnikov almost fell from it and looked down into the confused eyes of his partisan friend, looking back up at him from a contorted, stubbly face. Sotnikov just heard the words.

'Forgive me!'

'Go to hell!' snapped Sotnikov curtly.

It was time to end. Once again he sought the eyes of the motionless boy in the army cap. He stood as before, half a pace in front of the rest of the crowd, his eyes wide open in his pale face. Full of pain and fear his eyes were following someone moving along below the gallows, closer and closer to Sotnikov. Sotnikov did not know who was approaching him, but the face of the boy told him everything.

The log moved once more in Rybak's astonishingly weakened hands. Rybak was bending awkwardly, afraid, and apparently unable to carry out what he knew to be the most terrible thing that he had ever done. Somewhere behind Budila was bellowing in fury, and Sotnikov, in order to anticipate the inevitable, thrust the log from him with all the strength remaining in his good leg.

19

Rybak let go of the log and staggered back—Sotnikov's legs swung. by him, and knocked his hat into the snow. He stared back, but then bent down and grabbed his hat from below the hanged man, who was already swinging peacefully on his rope, describing a circle first in one direction, then in the other. Rybak could not bring himself to look at his face. He saw before his eyes only the legs swinging in the air—one foot in a tattered felt boot, and alongside it, its heel turned out, a filthy blueish foot with a stripe of dried blood on the ankle.

But the shock of what had happened didn't hold Rybak in its grip for long. By an effort of will he mastered his confusion and looked around. Beside Sotnikov and Demchikha the fifth rope hung unstretched—wasn't that still waiting for his neck?

But nothing happened to confirm his fears. Budila dragged the plywood packing case from beneath Demchikha and removed the bench from below the arch. From a distance Stas shouted something, but Rybak, still under the spell of the execution, either didn't understand or didn't hear distinctly what was said, and stood not knowing what to do. The group of Germans and civilians by the wall started to thin out—they were moving away, chatting, lighting cigarettes, all in a lively excited mood, as after a successfully completed, far from boring and even interesting piece of work. And then he began to believe, but still uncertainly—there, I've got away with it.

It did look as if he had escaped. They weren't going to hang him, he was going to live. The execution was over, the police cordon had withdrawn, and the people had been ordered to disperse, and the women, youngsters and the old people were moving away slowly, shattered and silent, on both sides of the street. Some of them paused briefly looking at the four hanging bodies, the women wiped

165

their eyes and hurried away. The *politsai* were tidying up round the gallows. Stas, his rifle as always on his shoulder, heaved the log from beneath the fifth noose, and again shouted something to Rybak. Again Rybak didn't hear, but guessed what was required of him and pulled the log from under Sotnikov and threw it under the fence. When he turned back, Stas was standing there with his usual white-toothed smile on his mask-like face, but his eyes remained wary and cold.

'Well, well! Good lad! Talented, too!' There was a sneer in the *politsai*'s praise, as he slapped Rybak on the shoulder with such force that he only just stayed on his feet, thinking, I could kill you, you bastard! But when he looked at Stas's sated, woodenly smiling face, Rybak smiled back, a twisted smile, only on his lips.

'And you thought I'd never be able to do it!'

'That's right! You proved me wrong! But you look pretty sick about it. Fancy feeling sorry for a bandit.'

Rybak gradually began to understand the full implication of what Stas had said, and a chilling feeling of a kind of guilt touched his mind. But he still didn't want to believe that he had had any part in the massacre—what had he done after all? Surely it wasn't him? Sotnikov had climbed up himself, and he'd kicked the log away himself. He had merely held the log steady. And even that he'd done under orders from the police.

The four bodies swung heavily on their long ropes, their heads on one side, their necks unnaturally twisted by the noose. One of the *politsai* had stuck up a piece of plywood with an inscription in Russian and German. Rybak didn't read what it said—he tried not to look at the gallows—the fifth empty noose terrified him. He thought that perhaps they would remove it from the arch but none of the *politsai* even went anywhere near it.

It looked as if it were all over. A guard had been posted by the gallows—a young long-necked *politsai* in an ankle-length grey coat, a rifle on his shoulder. The rest began to form up. So as not to be in the way, Rybak left the roadway and stood on the narrow snow-covered pavement, waiting to see what would happen next. His thoughts and feelings were deeply confused, his relief at his salvation was shadowed by something which he couldn't quite make out. Once again he was aware of an almost silenced voice, but a voice that was still insistent, urging him to make a break for it and lose himself in the forest. But for that he would have to pick the right moment. There was nothing to keep him here any more.

The *politsai* lined up in a column of threes, about fifteen of them. They were a motley bunch, some in new uniform greatcoats and caps, others in sheepskins, sweaters, and Red Army cast-offs. There was even one in a leather coat with the skirts cut off at the waist. Hardly anyone was left on the street now—there were just a few youngsters standing in the square, among them a thin, sickly looking boy in an army cap. His mouth half open, he was wrinkling his nose and staring at the gallows as if something worried him. A moment later he pointed a finger from one of his long sleeves across the street, and Rybak, who had half-turned away from him in embarrassment, stepped to one side so as to hide behind the rest of the *politsai*. The group was still lined up, cheerfully executing the bellowed orders of the one in charge, who was himself wholly immersed in the sweet joys of command and power, standing there with his elbows jutting out in the German fashion.

'Atten-tion!'

The *politsai* in the column moved as one and were still again. The senior officer ran a penetrating drill sergeant's eye down the ranks, until he spotted the lonely figure on the pavement.

'What d'you think you're doing? Get in line!'

Rybak was confused for a moment. The order gave him hope and worried him simultaneously. But there was no time to consider, and he hurriedly moved from the pavement and fell in at the tail of the column, next to a tall *politsai* in a fur hat, who looked at him with hostile eyes.

'Quick march!'

That was ordinary and familiar. Without thinking Rybak swung into step with the others, and had it not been for his empty hands, which he couldn't think what to do with, and the soiled white and blue armbands on the sleeves of his companions, he might have thought that he was back in the platoon with his own people.

They marched back along the same street they had come up. But this was quite a different journey. This time there was no dejection, no feeling of oppression—the people around him were lively, pleased with themselves, which was not, of course, surprising—he was among the victors. It might be for half a year, for a day or an hour, but these people felt on top of the world, warmed by the awareness that they had just wreaked total retribution, or perhaps that they had fully performed their duty. Some of them were

167

talking quietly, there were jokes and wisecracks, and no one once looked back at the arch. But everyone in the street was looking at them. The people who were coming away from the execution along the shabby walls and fences watched the local gang of traitors with a curse, with fear, with hate in the tear-reddened eyes of the women. But this did not disturb the *politsai* one whit. Perhaps it was just that they were used to it, and that they simply paid no heed to these frightened people who had been deprived of all their rights. Rybak thought with growing concern that he must make his escape. Perhaps there, at the turn of the road, he could leap the hedge and get out of town. It would be useful if there were a steep valley, or some undergrowth, or better still the forest. Or perhaps if he could get his hands on a horse.

The snow squeaked underfoot on the road as the *politsai* marched militarily along in step, with the senior officer walking along the pavement beside them, a slope-shouldered long faced man in a tightly belted police greatcoat. At his side he wore an army Nagan revolver in a low-slung holster with the brass showing where the leather had worn away. Beyond the bridge the leaders of the column checked their step and moved to the side—someone was driving towards them, and the *politsai* in charge bawled at him. Then the rest moved closer together, crushed up almost in their ranks. An old man driving an empty sleigh sluggishly yielded the road to them beneath the very windows of a cottage. Then Rybak suddenly had a real thought, he could leap into the sleigh, seize the reins and whip up the horse—he might just get away. But the old man! As he held back his young impatient horse, he cast a glance at the man in charge and at the whole column, and his eyes showed so deep a hatred for them that Rybak understood—no, he could never get away with it! But who would be willing to help him? Then, thunderstruck, he was swamped by the unexpected realisation that there was no way of getting out of it. After this execution there was nowhere to go. There was no way of escape from the column he had joined.

The shattering clarity of this revelation jolted him so much that he stumbled, fell out of step and couldn't pick up the rhythm again.

'What's up with you?' his neighbour asked in a scornful bass voice.

'Nothing!'

'You're not used to it then? You'll learn!'

Rybak didn't reply, realising very clearly that all idea of escape had vanished, and that his part in this execution had bound him inseparably to the Germans and their Russian henchmen. Although his body was still alive, a large part of him had been liquidated along with the four on the gallows.

Yes, there was no going back to the past now. Now he was everyone's enemy, and his own enemy as well.

Confused and anxious, he couldn't make sense of what had happened, nor decide whose fault it was. The Germans? The war? The *politsai*? He longed intensely to avoid admitting his own guilt, and tried to lay the blame on other people, or on the times or the circumstances. For indeed, what was he guilty of himself? He hadn't chosen this fate for himself, had he? And had he not fought till the bitter end? He had fought harder and more stubbornly than that ambitious Sotnikov. Indeed Sotnikov bore more of the blame than anyone else for the position that Rybak now found himself in. If Sotnikov hadn't been ill, if he hadn't been hit by that bullet, if he hadn't needed so much looking after, Rybak would have been safely back in the forest long ago. And now Sotnikov, swinging in his noose from the arch, couldn't give a damn about anyone else, while Rybak, although alive, was much the worse off.

Totally bewildered, his mind enveloped in an impenetrable fog, Rybak marched with the column to the familiar gates of the *politsai* headquarters. They were brought to a halt in the yard, and on the word of command turned to face the porch. The chief, the interrogator Portnov, and the two in German uniform were already standing there. The senior *politsai* reported their arrival loudly, and the chief cast a carping eye over the column.

'At ease! Twenty minutes break,' he said. His eyes sought out Rybak. 'You, come and see me!'

'Yes, sir!', Rybak rapped back, shrinking from something unavoidable, which had now caught right up with him.

His neighbour jabbed his elbow into his side.

'*Jawohl*, not "Yes, Sir!" You'll have to get used to it.'

Rybak thought, Go to hell, all of them, to hell and the devil! For good!

The column was dismissed. Rybak looked around him in confusion, wondering what he could do. The *politsai* in the yard were chattering noisily, skylarking about, cursing one another playfully, lighting up, and the sweet smell of cigarette smoke floated in the air. Some of them went into the building, and one went off into the corner of the yard to the narrow plank hut with two doors on wooden hinges. Rybak set off there as well.

'Hey, where are you off to?'

'Shan't be a moment.'

It appeared that he had spoken calmly enough to conceal what he saw now as his only way out, and Stas turned away unconcernedly. Yes, the hell with them, the people and everything else. Rybak slammed shut the squeaking door, fastened it with the wire loop, and looked up. The ceiling was low, but high enough for his purpose. There was a piece of roofing felt sticking through a gap in the planks in the roof, and the gap would be quite enough to push his belt through. He resolutely unfastened his sheepskin—and suddenly froze. There was no belt on his trousers. He had forgotten that it had been taken from him the previous day before he was put into his cell. His hands ran over his clothing in search of some alternative, but there was nothing that would serve.

On the other side of the partition there were heavy footsteps and the door scraped to. His last chance of getting even with fate had gone. Boundless despair welled up within him and he all but broke into an outburst of sobbing.

But a familiar voice from outside restored his self control.

'Are you going to be much longer?' Stas shouted from a distance.

'Coming now.'

'The chief wants you!'

Of course the chief wouldn't tolerate delay. When the bosses whistle, you jump to it. The more so if you've decided to become a *politsai*. Yesterday he had dreamt of that as a salvation. Today the fulfilment of that dream had turned out to be a catastrophe.

Rybak blew his nose, looked abstractly at a button, and fastened his sheepskin. It looked now as if there were nothing he could do—that's fate. The capricious fate of man caught up in war. No longer able to think of anything else to do, he released the catch, and trying to master his confusion, stepped out of the lavatory.

On the threshold, eyeing him impatiently, stood the chief of the *politsai*.

ABOUT THE AUTHOR

Vasil Bykov has had two novels published, both in *Novy Mir,* the magazine of the Soviet Writers Union. His first, *The Dead Feel No Pain,* was attacked for slandering the Soviet Army. *The Ordeal* was published in Russia in 1970.